What people are saying about …

CH•

"This book defies normal boundaries. It is not merely biblical fiction, nor is the diary structure all that important. What you have in your hands is a truly astonishing novel. Ginger Garrett shows great originality and even greater promise."

Davis Bunn, best-selling author

"A story that is sure to be a classic! Exciting, dramatic, and filled with truth. A great read from the first page!"

Bodie and Brock Thoene, best-selling authors of the Zion Covenant Series and the A.D. Chronicles

"An exciting novel from a talented author."

Karen Kingsbury, best-selling author of *Shades of Blue*

"Chosen is a richly detailed retelling of Queen Esther's story. The brave Jewish woman comes alive on the pages of a diary that will leave you wondering if the words are actually the queen's or Ms. Garrett's. A gem of a read."

Carol Umberger, author of the award-winning Scottish Crown series

"Ginger sweeps the sands of time from this figure of ancient history and gives her a voice once again—and what a compelling voice it is! To revisit this ancient story is to gain a vision for the contemporary world."

Siri L. Mitchell, author of *Love's Pursuit* and *Moon Over Tokyo*

CHOSEN

CHOSEN
THE LOST DIARIES
OF QUEEN
ESTHER

LOST LOVES OF THE BIBLE
BOOK ONE

GINGER GARRETT

David C Cook
transforming lives together

CHOSEN
Published by David C. Cook
4050 Lee Vance View
Colorado Springs, CO 80918 U.S.A.

David C. Cook Distribution Canada
55 Woodslee Avenue, Paris, Ontario, Canada N3L 3E5

David C. Cook U.K., Kingsway Communications
Eastbourne, East Sussex BN23 6NT, England

David C. Cook and the graphic circle C logo
are registered trademarks of Cook Communications Ministries.

The Web site addresses recommended throughout this book are offered as a
resource to you. These Web sites are not intended in any way to be or imply an
endorsement on the part of David C. Cook, nor do we vouch for their content.

This story is a work of fiction. All characters and events are the product of the author's
imagination. Any resemblance to any person, living or dead, is coincidental.

All Scripture quotations, unless otherwise noted, are taken from the *Holy Bible,
New International Version*. *NIV*. Copyright © 1973, 1978, 1984 by International
Bible Society. Used by permission of Zondervan. All rights reserved.

LCCN 2009943354
ISBN 978-1-4347-6801-8
eISBN 978-0-7814-0427-3

© 2010 Ginger Garrett
Ginger Garrett is represented by MacGregor Literary.
First edition published by NavPress in 2005 © Ginger Garrett, ISBN 1-57683-651-7

The Team: Terry Behimer, Ramona Tucker, Amy Kiechlin,
Jaci Schneider, Sarah Schultz, and Karen Athen
Cover Design: DogEared Design, Kirk DouPonce
Cover photos: iStockphoto, royalty-free

Printed in the United States of America
Second Edition 2010

1 2 3 4 5 6 7 8 9 10

122809

Acknowledgments

Many people have contributed to the effort to bring the diaries to the public: In addition to the team at David C. Cook, we wish to thank Rachelle Gardner, Nicci Jordan Hubert, and Andrea Christian. An Advisory Panel was established with Dale Slaton and Sherrill McCracken as first readers, and included numerous contributors. For everyone who contributed insight or expertise, thank you.

Note to the Reader

These diaries, reproduced here in their entirety, were dated using an ancient Babylonian calendar. Explanation must be given so that the modern reader is not confused. Three dates are given at the top of each entry, including: month, the year of the king's reign, and the year after creation. Ancient calendars, of course, did not include the markers "BC," "AD," "BCE," or "CE." The "number of years after creation" was only a very rough estimate determined by early Jewish priests, using key historical dates given in the first inspired Scriptures.

The months were lunar months. At the first report from two reliable witnesses that a full moon had risen, the first day of the next month was declared. The months correspond roughly to ours, although their New Year began later:

Nisan	April
Iyyar	May
Sivan	June
Tammuz	July
Av	August
Elul	September

Tishri	October
Kheshvan	November
Kislev	December
Tevet	January
Shevat	February
Adar	March
Adar II	A leap year, occurring approximately every 3 years

In addition to understanding this dating system, we would like to call to your attention the special features we have added for further study and interest. The Persian Antiquities Authority has graciously allowed us to include news reports and academic commentary in an appendix to the diaries. We hope this will allow you, the reader, to better place these diaries in the context of Esther's world, and your own. We've indicated these features with a footnote to direct you to the corresponding article in the appendix.

INTRODUCTION

In September 1939, Hitler launches an unprovoked attack in Poland and begins his reign of terror. His first public proclamation after the invasion closes all synagogues, effective on the first day of the festival of Purim. Purim is the Jewish holiday that celebrates the heroism of one woman, Esther, and her triumph against the evil of Jewish genocide. Hitler was crafting a horrific annihilation for his Jewish captives, and Purim would give them a shining hope that the courage of even one woman might still be enough to stop him.

Hitler's men raced against time to destroy the synagogues and wipe the festival of Purim from the mind of every Jew. "Unless Germany is victorious," Hitler shrieked to his men, "Jews could then celebrate a second triumphant Purim festival!" Hitler may have hated the entire race, but he feared one woman. Even her dusty memory could threaten his bloody regime. Who was this woman who gave a madman pause? Could she even now call to her people across the centuries?

FROM THEARTNEWSPAPER.COM, INTERNATIONAL EDITION

LONDON AND PARIS MARKETS FLOODED WITH LOOTED IRANIAN ANTIQUITIES

REPORT ON JANUARY 2001 DISCOVERY

BY EDEK OSSER[1]

JIROFT, IRAN. In January 2001 a group of Iranians from Jiroft in the southwest province of Kerman stumbled upon an ancient tomb. Inside they found hoards of objects decorated with highly distinctive engravings of animals, mythological figures, and architectural motifs.

They did not realise it at the time, but they had just made one of the most remarkable archaeological discoveries in recent years.

A few weeks after the discovery, officials from Iran's Ministry of Culture, vastly outnumbered by the local people, watched hopelessly as thousands systematically dug up the area. The locals set up a highly organised impromptu system to manage the looting: each family was allocated an equal plot of six-metres to dig.

This organised pillaging continued for an entire year. Dozens of tombs were discovered, some containing up to 60 objects, and thousands of ancient objects were removed.

---

1 We wish to thank the *Art Newspaper*, International Edition, for its kind permission to use this excerpt.

WAR ON TERROR CLAIMS UNINTENDED VICTIMS

FEBRUARY 2003

The war on terror is wreaking havoc on archaeology across the Middle East, threatening the oldest sites with destruction from both bombs and looters. Across the world, archaeologists of all faiths and political ideologies are banding together to protect the most valuable sites.

"These sites contain historical artifacts dating back 5,500 years," says one expert, who was struggling to guard an ancient grave that looters had already damaged. As he watched, a child sifted through a pile of rubbish, looking for smaller finds missed by the professional looters.

The war on terror may be making the world a safer place, but it is destroying the written record of civilization. What bombs do not destroy, greed does. Governments focused on eliminating terrorists and protecting civilians do not have the additional resources to send armed guards to protect known archaeological digs. When a bomb hits an area and a relic is discovered in the rubble, looters arrive within hours to strip the site clean, often selling their finds on Internet auctions.

One archaeologist has spent the last six months cataloging license plate numbers instead of relics. He hopes to one day bring justice to his country, and the antiquities back.

"Cars and rented trucks hover around these sites like vultures," he says, "even backing up right into the middle of the dig and loading up."

Archaeologists watch helplessly as these "artifact mercenaries," sometimes armed with guns, saw up larger statues for easy transport, dumping gold jewelry and pottery alike into the beds of the trucks before speeding away.

And people of all income levels are getting involved. To families ravaged by war, one artifact can put food on the table for months. For diplomats, a gift to a contributor's private art collection can assure political support and continued financial contributions.

U.S. AGENCY FOR INTERNATIONAL DEVELOPMENT

BUREAU FOR DEMOCRACY, CONFLICT, AND HUMANITARIAN ASSISTANCE (DCHA)

OFFICE OF U.S. FOREIGN DISASTER ASSISTANCE (OFDA)

DECEMBER 29, 2003

On December 26, 2003, at 5:27 a.m. local time, an earthquake struck Kerman Province in southeastern Iran. According to the U.S. Geological Survey, the earthquake measured 6.6 on the Richter scale and had a depth of 10 km. The epicenter was near the city of Bam, 180 km southeast of the provincial capital of Kerman and 975 km southeast of Tehran.

The United Nations Office for the Coordination of Humanitarian Affairs (UN OCHA) reports that an estimated 100,000 to 120,000 people live in Bam and the surrounding villages, all of whom have been affected by the earthquake.

International media reports estimate that the earthquake has resulted in the deaths of 20,000 to 30,000 people.

Government of Iran (GOI) officials estimate that 25,000 to 40,000 have been injured. GOI officials report that 80 percent of houses have been destroyed in the immediate area of Bam, and an estimated 70,000 residents are homeless.

MARCH 4, 2004

FOR IMMEDIATE RELEASE

ANCIENT DIARIES OF QUEEN ESTHER ACQUIRED

A twelve-year-old Iranian girl has offered for sale the publication rights to a box of antiquities, which include the sealed scrolls believed to be the personal diaries of Queen Esther, who ruled in Persia approximately 480–465 BC.

The owner will not say how she came into possession of the artifacts. She was discovered by humanitarian workers after the December earthquake, wandering in the streets with the box and a few belongings. It was understood that her family was killed by the earthquake and she was seeking to sell the box to pay for transportation to another city to live with relatives.

The diaries, which are recorded on scrolls in Aramaic, the adopted language of the ancient Persian Empire, could bring in at least $130 million at auction.

Although it is difficult at this time to verify all details, media outlets have reported that the girl is now living outside of Iran, possibly in Paris with an unnamed relief worker, and has successfully negotiated with her former government to place the scrolls in Iran's national museum. Conditional to the museum acquiring the scrolls, they will be duplicated and published for public review. All royalties will be payable to the girl, who will also retain all future publication rights.

PROLOGUE

Fourth Day of the Month of Av
Year 3414 after Creation

If you have opened this, you are the chosen one.

For this book has been sealed in the tomb of the ancients of Persia, never to be opened, I pray, until G-d[1] has put His finger on a new woman of destiny, a woman who will rise up and change her nation. But we will not talk of your circumstances, and the many reasons this book may have fallen into your hands. There are no mistakes with prayer. You have indeed been called. If this sounds too strange, if you must look around your room and question whether G-d's finger has perhaps slipped, if you are not a woman with the means to change a nation, then join me on a journey. You must return with me now to a place without hope, a nation that had lost sight of G-d, a girl with nothing to offer, and no one to give it to.

I must introduce myself first as I truly am: an exiled Jew, and an orphan. My given name was Hadassah, but the oppression of exile

---

1 Out of respect for God, Jews write the name of God without the vowels, believing that the name of God is too holy to be written out completely by a human. God is referred to as either "G-d" or "YHVH."

has stripped that too from me: I am now called Esther,[2] so that I may blend in with my captors. My people, the Hebrew nation, had been sent out of our homeland after a bitter defeat in battle. We were allowed to settle in the kingdom of Persia, but we were not allowed to truly prosper there. We blended in, our lives preserved, but our heritage and customs were forced underground. Our hearts, once set only on returning to Jerusalem, were set out to wither in the heat of the Arabian sun. My cousin Mordecai rescued me when I was orphaned and we lived in the capital city of Susa, under the reign of King Xerxes.[3] Mordecai had a small flock of sheep that I helped tend, and we sold their fleece in the market. If times were good, we would sell a lamb for someone's celebration. It was always for others to celebrate. We merely survived. But Mordecai was kind and good, and I was not forced into dishonor like the other orphans I had once known. This is how my story begins, and I give you these details not for sympathy, but so you will know that I am a girl well acquainted with bitter reality. I am not given to the freedom in flights of fantasy. But how can I explain to you the setting of my story? It is most certainly far removed from your experience. For I suspect that in the future, women will know freedom. And freedom is not an easy thing to forget, even if only to entertain an orphan's story.

But you must forget now. I was born into a world, and into this story, where even the bravest women were faceless specters. Once married, they could venture out of their homes only with veils and escorts. No one yet had freed our souls. Passion and pleasure, like

---

2 The name Esther is related to the Persian name of Ishtar, a pagan goddess of the stars.
3 Esther refers to the king by his Persian name. In the Hebrew texts of antiquity, he is also referred to as Ahasuerus.

freedom, were the domain of men, and even young girls knew the wishes of their hearts would always be subject to a man's desire for wealth. A man named Pericles summed up my time so well in his famed oration: "The greatest glory of a woman is to be least talked about by men, whether they are praising you or criticizing you."

Our role was clear: We were to be objects of passion, to receive a man's attention mutely, and to respond only with children for the estate. Even the most powerful woman of our time, the beautiful Queen Vashti, was powerless. That was my future as a girl and I dared not lift my eyes above its horizon. That is how I enter this story. But give me your hand and let us walk back now, past the crumbling walls of history, to this world forgotten but a time yet remembered. Let me tell you the story of a girl unspared, plunged into heartache and chaos, who would save a nation.

My name is Esther, and I will be queen.

Eleventh Day of Shevat
Third Year of the Reign of Xerxes
Year 3394 after Creation

Was it today that I became fully awake, or have I only now begun to dream? Today Cyrus saw me in the marketplace haggling gently with my favorite shopkeeper, Shethana, over the price of a fleece. Shethana makes the loveliest rugs—I think they are even more lovely than the ones imported from the East—and her husband is known for his skill in crafting metals of all kinds. When I turned fifteen last year, he fashioned for me a necklace with several links in the center, painted various shades of blue. He says it is an art practiced in Egypt, this inlaying of colors into metal shapes. I feel so exotic with it on and wear it almost daily. I know it is as close to adventure as Mordecai will ever allow.

But as Shethana and I haggled over the fleece, both of us smiling because she knew I would as soon give it to her, Cyrus walked by eating a flatbread he had purchased from another vendor. He grimaced when he took a bite—I think he might have gotten a very strong taste of shallot—and I laughed. He laughed back, wiping his eyes with his jacket and fanning his mouth, and then, oh then, his gaze held my eyes for a moment. Everything in my body seemed to come alive suddenly and I felt afraid, for my legs couldn't stand as straight and steady and I couldn't get my mouth to work. Shethana noticed right away and didn't conceal her grin as she glanced between Cyrus and me. I should have doubled the price of her fleece right then!

Cyrus turned to walk away, and I tried to focus again on my transaction. I could not meet Shethana's eyes now—I didn't want to be questioned about men and marriage, for everyone knows I have no dowry. To dream of winning Cyrus would be as foolish as to run my own heart straight through. I cannot dream, for it will surely crush me. And yet I can't stop this warm flood that sweeps over me when he is near.

I haven't told you the best part—when Shethana bought her fleece and left, I allowed myself to close my eyes for a moment in the heat of the day, and when I opened them again, there was a little stack of flatbread in my booth. I looked in every direction but could see no one. Taking a bite, I had to spit it out and started laughing. Cyrus was right—the vendor used many bitter shallots. The flatbread was a disaster.

2

Once more I can tell you of exciting events!

King Xerxes has proclaimed a feast that will last for 180 days. It is for the royals of his provinces, every satrap and governor. Of course, no one in the market will go, as we are all common, but the feast has brought us to life nonetheless. Some of the customers in the marketplace have whispered to me that the feast is to bring support for Xerxes' coming invasion of Greece. Greece would be the final crown jewel for Persia; all else has been captured. But the Greeks are a difficult people to conquer. Persia has made shallow progress at moments, but never won her war. The Spartans are fierce warriors but even their softer cousins, the Athenians, will defend her shores to the death. Greeks are deeply superstitious, and this makes them irresistible bait for the ruthless Persians. The Greeks will not fight during religious festivals, even with an approaching army. I know Persia is hungry for more land. We are not burdened by their gods and we care not when we strike. No one here believes the Greek gods hold any sway over our fortunes. So the men say, "Let the Greeks worship as they must, and we'll take their land even as they pray inside their temples." As a Jew in exile here, I cannot bring myself to pray victory for either side. How foolish they seem to me, worshipping gods made from mud and stone, when our houses are made from no less!

But Mordecai tells me darker news—the Jewish elders suspect the feast is being given to remind us that our exile has been declared finished for years now. Yet so many of us remain, unable or unwilling to make the journey home yet! They say Xerxes and his officials want to make it clear to the kingdom of Persia that the G-d of Israel has either forgotten His people or abandoned them to Persia forever. I don't know why Xerxes would want to humiliate the Jews, however. This is a land of many gods—surely no one has paid so much notice to the one G-d the exiles still worship?

Mordecai and his officials are watching the palace carefully for a sign of what is to come. It has been mentioned more than once that perhaps my people will be taken as slaves at the end of the feast, when it has been made clear to everyone that this G-d does not reign in the hearts of the Jews here anymore. One man harassed Mordecai in the market, telling him, "If you have chosen Persia as your home, you must serve Persia as your master." I can tell Mordecai shares the fears of the elders but has not come to a conclusion. "Perhaps the feast is just a feast," he says. "Xerxes is known for his appetites." The crown has brought Xerxes unlimited access to food and women and war, and he has not restrained himself.

So for days now I have been watching caravans move through the city, weighted down with wines, pistachios, dates, and so many delicacies that it's all I can do to swallow down my salted goat meat at night. I wonder if Mordecai, too, longs for just one package to fall from the caravan, unnoticed; but then he's too busy counting his money from the market. We've sold nearly all of our lambs to the palace for the great feast with their promises of extra money if we can deliver more tender meats before the feast is ended. The palace commissioner even spied the red roses I have growing outside our door and asked what price I would take for the blooms. I set a fair price. It is not such a burden to send a bit of my heart to the palace. Perhaps I will catch scent of my roses later and they would bring me news of the rarities I was missing!

3

Today at the market I caught sight of Cyrus moving slowly through the booths with his father and mother. His mother is a good customer of mine. She has an eye for the best cuts of meat and occasionally even takes a bloom from the roses I sell. I know she must grow her own, but I think she buys from me because she knows I am an orphan. It doesn't feel like sympathy, though. It feels a little more like a certain kindness. I waited for her to come to my booth and was paralyzed by the sight of Cyrus today! I had to stand there and conduct my business, but I felt clumsy, even when I wasn't moving.

Then a strange thing happened, and I do not know what to make of it. Perhaps as I write, its meaning will become clear to me. Cyrus's father made the purchase this time, and he was all business. Cyrus held back with his mother, but I could feel him looking at me from behind her robes. I got the feeling I was being inspected by this father even as he inspected the goods in my booth. I do not know if this is a bad omen or a hint of something good to come. Cyrus's father gave me no clue. He bought his meat and left without another word. I noticed he exchanged a glance with Mordecai as Mordecai approached the booth to let me rest for lunch. But Mordecai can tell me nothing of what my future may hold. I wish he would listen more to the women's gossip in the booths of the market—for they would know what was unfolding. But Mordecai's ears are dull to the details of what's really important in the life of a girl.

I try to pray at night, facing Jerusalem with Mordecai, who whispers the sacred texts in his prayers. I do not whisper my own prayers aloud, but I wonder if our G-d hears the prayers of orphans as readily as He hears the prayers of great men like my Mordecai. It is not for me to suggest, but if I am ever given in marriage, I want it to be to a kind and gentle boy, like Cyrus. But in all I must remain silent, my prayers sent with closed eyes and an unmoving mouth.

4

First Day of Tishri
Fifth Year of the Reign of Xerxes
Year 3396 after Creation

Our new year is beginning today, while the king's great feast is almost over. He has now opened the palace gates for all men of Persia to come and enjoy the splendors and wines of his garden. The beautiful Queen Vashti has opened her palace as well—every woman in the province is welcome. Vashti is the most beautiful woman in the world. No one can dispute that about her when Xerxes has had his pick from every nation and every tribe. It is said to look upon her is to be left breathless, that to look into her eyes is to see the sapphires of all the earth, and her teeth are endless rows of perfect pearls, that no sunrise has ever matched the spreading glory of her long hair. (I want so badly to go and see her myself, to learn how she does command the imagination of so many men.)

I wish I were old enough to attend! I begged Mordecai last night over and over, but he won't hear of it. He's angry enough that the palace has set the opening date of both feasts on our day of holy rest and the palace has also consigned many Jews to work at the feast. A rumor ran through our village that the palace was using serving utensils that had been stolen from our Temple when it was first destroyed and never returned. I didn't believe that, though—who would be so bold?

"It's just once," I pleaded to Mordecai, "and we could attend to our duties in the morning before leaving."

Mordecai shook his head.

"I'll never have a chance again to go inside the queen's palace!" I protested to deaf old ears. I'm so angry at Mordecai, but all I can do is hold my tongue, my anger softened by the fact that he rescued me long ago. I know if it wasn't for me, Mordecai would have a better chance at marrying. He could save more money for the bride price he must give and more freely consider his future. I've seen him secreting money away into a jar every night after the market. For the longest time I thought it was to buy a bride, but now I suspect it is for a dowry for me. Has he seen the looks that pass between Cyrus and me at market? Has G-d answered my prayers through my uncle?

Mordecai is so good to me. But stubborn. I'll never change his mind about the queen's feast.

So tonight I lie on my bed dreaming of adventures I have been denied once again. I have to shut my ears to the sounds of the lyres, the tambourines, and the women from my village laughing as they make their way to the palace. When, Lord, when will I have adventures and attend glorious feasts? Must all my days be spent on flocks and flowers and grinding flour for our dinner? Will it be my lot to always dream and never live?[1]

---

1 See corresponding commentary on page 273, "The Women of the Bible: Our Sisters, Our Selves."

5

Second Day of Tishri
Fifth Year of the Reign of Xerxes
Year 3396 after Creation

Today I am sixteen, and I should not even write down the events of the day. If Mordecai ever finds this, if this book ever sees eyes beyond my own, I will burn with shame. But without a mother, I have no one to tell these things to, and so I must write them down here. A girl cannot keep such things to herself, for I feel I would burst! I do tell them to G-d in my prayers, and I am emboldened when Mordecai places his hand over mine as we pray together. I believe more and more that G-d will bend low and hear. But some prayers remain silent, and some thoughts must not be shared with my good cousin.

Cyrus, although the same age as I, celebrated his passage into manhood when he was but thirteen. The elders of the city, including Mordecai, took Cyrus to the hills where, Mordecai tells me, he hunted and killed a wild ram and the men feasted on it by a campfire, and took turns blessing Cyrus as he began his journey into manhood. I knew of these events only through Mordecai, although I envied Mordecai almost to sickness for the privilege of spending this time, and that meal, with Cyrus. My Cyrus. I can call him that now, with certainty, for we have exchanged more than looks today! Oh, let me tell you of the most marvelous day a girl has ever had!

There is no celebration for the Jewish girls in this village who pass into womanhood, although everyone knows we become women earlier than the boys become men! So today in the market, as I did every year, I had to content myself with receiving many warm hugs from the women, and a few trinkets to mark the day. My heart burned to be acknowledged like Cyrus was. Am I forever fated to be a child? Will no one accept me as the adult I surely am?

But perhaps that is what it means to be a woman, to carry these little wounds in your heart and make no mention of them. Still, it was a good day and it brought good gifts. Shethana's husband sent along a beautiful engraving with a picture of the Temple, which had been destroyed before our captivity. It was the dream of rebuilding this Temple that had kept my people alive in their hearts for so long. There had never been a greater treasure for my people than the dream of rebuilding this Temple in Jerusalem, and so while we made our beds here in this foreign land of gold and swords, we never truly lived here. I love the engraving. Others sent a few sweets and a small jar of scented water. I know it is not as dear as real perfume, but who could ever dream a shepherd girl and shopkeeper would have perfume! Scented water is fitting, and enough. So it was a lovely day. People were not so quick to haggle over my prices in the market, and a few overpaid just by a bit, with a twinkle in their eyes. I felt loved. My mother would have been pleased with the day, I thought.

As the sun began to edge away, and vendors packed and left, I was reluctant to leave, somehow. I knew Mordecai would be at home, waiting, and we would share a small meal and our best wishes for the future before going to sleep, but I felt lonely. I think I was missing my mother and father. Everyone in the village had been so kind, so kind and good, yet it only made me miss being loved that much more. I hated the heaviness that crept into my heart as I folded our tent and turned for home. When my throat began to burn and a tear ran down my cheek, I knew it was more than the hot sands I was walking upon. I could not raise my head from the sadness of being so loved in the village … and so alone in my heart.

Then he was there. Cyrus. He just stood in the road, watching as my shuffling feet marked their way to him. I froze for a moment— how could something you have dreamed of for so long strike you so completely dumb? I had rehearsed a moment alone with him for months, yet here it was, and I was at a loss. I simply stared. He smiled and walked toward me. When I still could not find my voice, he took the tent from my arms and set it on the ground. He reached for my hand and led me toward the mountain to our east.[1] We walked side by side in silence, his hand never leaving mine, until we were on a beautiful perch, with a view of the palace in the distance, and the moon rising slowly over the glittering gold exterior. Cyrus turned me gently to face him and kissed me softly, just once, on the lips. I have never been kissed on the lips. It was so sweet, so soft, and set a fire in my belly that I could not have expected. Everything in me seemed alive, and I could feel my heart pounding, and the blood rushing in

---

1 It is unclear which mountain Esther would be referring to here. Susa was located just outside the dramatic mountain range of the Zagros mountains, and Iran is a country with extreme terrains.

my veins. Mordecai surely would have stoned us both if he caught us, yet all I could think of was another kiss.

Instead, Cyrus spoke. "The elders have spoken to my father. I am told to plan for my future." He looked off into the night before continuing. "In another year, I will take a wife. And I can think of no one but you, Esther."

I could not believe my ears. It was as if my heart had written his words.

He frowned and looked at me with seriousness. "I know you have no dowry, and although Mordecai is highly respected among our people, my father respects gold above all else. I do not know yet how we can be together, Esther, but I do know you will not be taken from me. Not for a matter of gold. I pledge that I will be by your side for eternity. But if you feel differently about me, if you cannot return my love, tell me now."

He was giving me a courteous exit! It made me sick and giddy all at once.

I slid my hand back into his. I leaned my head against his neck and wished to stay there forever. He was so warm, and his skin seemed so roughened and different; he was the most intoxicating wine I had ever drunk. I understood why some people in the village had taken to their cups and never returned. There are some moments that change you forever, and some tastes that will never leave your tongue. I was drunk indeed with all these emotions. I would never be the same.

Cyrus smiled as he held me away from him and led me again down the mountain. Although it was quite dark now, he waited behind and gave me a nudge toward the road and my forgotten tent.

"Go now," he told me, "get home and say nothing while I work this out. I do not know how it will come to pass, but have faith that we will be together."

So I picked up my tent and hurried home. I do not even know when he quit watching me and went to his own home. I seemed to feel his eyes watching me all night, this acute awareness of him being so near. I wondered if I looked any different, if the blush had yet left my cheeks. But if wise old Mordecai knew anything had changed about me, he didn't say. He blamed my distraction and lateness on the excitement of reaching sixteen, and on the trinkets I had received throughout my day. Oh, but Mordecai, if I could only tell you, the greatest treasure was not what I received, but what I had given away! For my heart was gone and belonged to Cyrus alone.

I remember now what the rabbi has told us about the creation of the world, about the plan for a man and a woman. The blessed Scriptures tell us that "for this reason, a child will leave his mother and father, and marry, and the two will become one." I stared out my window and I knew this was, somehow, my mother's gift to me on my birthday. She and Father had been heavy on my heart all day, being so near in thought that their absence had crushed my spirit. But I knew now that it was time to leave them and become one with another. I leaned out my window and whispered to them among the stars, "Good night, Mother. Good night, Father. I know it is time to let you go and embrace my new love. I will look for you again on the shores of heaven. Watch over me as I make my way to my destiny."

A shooting star caught my eye, and I wept, and smiled.

6

Mordecai tossed the bulletin at my feet while I ground our flour outside at the common stone, the grinding stone we shared with the other houses close to ours, preparing for a meal to celebrate the new year. Cyrus and I had only exchanged glances in the market for the past several weeks, and I was anxious for time to pass. I stopped to wipe my hands before picking it up.

> *By proclamation of the king, let it be known that*
> *Queen Vashti has been banished from her throne,*
> *and from the King's presence, for her rebellion. A new*
> *queen will be found, one who knows her place and*
> *gives honor to the king. Let it also be known that in*
> *every house, every man is to be the master, and his*
> *word shall be law for those living under his roof.*

I looked up at Mordecai, who was smiling.

"What does this mean, Cousin?" I asked.

Mordecai crouched near me, retrieving the bulletin from my hand. "Esther, during the feast that Xerxes and Vashti threw, the one I forbade you to attend, there was much drunken debauchery. Xerxes sent word for Vashti to parade herself before all the common men in attendance in the garden. Ah, women are always getting into trouble in a garden, wouldn't you say?"

I rolled my eyes at his weak humor.

And then he leaned in close and whispered in a somber tone, "Xerxes commanded Vashti to appear wearing her royal crown."

"And what is so awful about that?" I asked.

Mordecai held his words for a moment, for effect. "She was to wear her crown and nothing else," he finally answered.

I lost my balance on my haunches and sat abruptly in the sand.

Mordecai rolled the bulletin and tapped me on the head with it, laughing. "You see, your cousin Mordecai did well to keep you at home. Who knows what else went on there? Wine flowing freely among frightened men is never a good idea."

"You mean frightened of the coming war with Greece?" I asked.

Mordecai laughed again. "Worse than that, my child; they are afraid of their women. These men who would draw their swords without a second thought are frightened of the invisible weapons their women wield behind closed doors! You see, the women in Athens have been crying out for a taste of that country's democracy, and so the women of Xerxes' rule are getting restless as well. You've seen that his customs, and the customs of this land, are much different for women from our own Hebrew tradition. Women here are carried away to harems, entire palaces filled with concubines, never to see the light of day again. What goes on inside the harems, we can only guess at. The only god in Persia is pleasure, pleasure that is often at the expense of women."

Mordecai was frowning now. He did not like living among these "godless people," as he called them. I thought that was a funny description, for I have never seen so many gods. There are small carved idols everywhere, in homes and in the market, in carriages and in the fields. If you have enough money, you can buy any god you'd like. I wondered why the G-d of the Hebrews would send us into exile to this kingdom. Sometimes I was jealous of my friends in the market who could carry their gods in their pockets. It would make G-d seem nearer if I could but touch and feel Him. Mordecai says this is the meaning of faith: to see without sight, to believe against reason that G-d is near, and that He rules in the affairs of men. And orphans.

"So if he conquers Greece, he will not take a queen there," I speculated. "But where will he find his new bride?"[1]

---

1 See corresponding commentary of page 275 of the appendix.

7

Second Day of the Month of Sivan
Sixth Year of the Reign of Xerxes
Year 3397 after Creation

I have only a moment tonight before Mordecai insists I blow out my candle. I had to tell you, faithful diary, of the terrible loss we have suffered in the village! During the night, several of us lost lambs to a hateful predator. Most probably a mountain lion,[1] Mordecai told me, judging from the terrible gashes along the necks of a few carcasses, and the dragging marks through the sands. These lions like to kill at the neck and then drag their supper away. We have only lost two lambs, but Mordecai says our neighbor has lost several more. How could one lion be so hungry, and so violent? It is a mystery to me, and one I mean to ask Mordecai about, how a world so full of G-d's grace could be so full of his wrath, as well.

The villagers, however, believe the bloody work was done by Lamashtu.[2] She is angered, they say, because the women secretly wear

---

1 In the time of Esther, many species of big cats, including lions, flourished in the region.
2 Lamashtu was a demon who ate babies. Her rival in the underworld was Pazuzu, and women wore the image of Pazuzu to protect their unborn. This belief system made it possible to explain miscarriages and the high infant mortality rate.

amulets of Pazuzu. Since Xerxes commanded the worship of Ahura Mazda, people have been more discreet in their worship of other gods. Meanwhile, the villagers believe Lamashtu is hungry for children and will soon grow tired of our livestock. Soon, they say, she will begin devouring the children of the village, and not even the amulets will save them. (How simple my own faith seems now compared to these many warring demons and gods of the underworld! I have only to learn one name, YHVH, and follow Him with all my heart.)

The stories from the village make Mordecai laugh. There is no danger for the children of the village, he says, unless they fall asleep at their chores!

I would tell you more news, and more news of Cyrus, but the hour is late and I hear Mordecai calling to me. Good night. Pray safety for our flocks while we sleep.

8

Sixteenth Day of the Month of Av
Sixth Year of the Reign of Xerxes
Year 3397 after Creation

It is frustrating to have so little scroll to record my thoughts. I know of no other girl in Susa who can even write, so I am spoiled even in this by Mordecai. But would that I had unlimited space to record all my adventures in the market! You must forgive me, diary, for so few entries. I conserve the scroll for events I dream of telling my own daughters about.

I continue to see Cyrus in the market, but we are rarely alone. His mother or father always tend to the family's shopping, and often I must be content to only exchange glances with my love. Twice now we have met after the market's close and escaped to the mountain in the east and had a moment of peace together. Although it's not really peace, for everything in me battles at once; the urgency of wanting a kiss, my words tumbling out too fast, and my heart skipping beats like a street musician who loses time at all the wrong places. Really, everything in me goes wrong. I suppose, without a mother to guide me in matters of marriage, everything in me must fumble in ignorance as I do.

This year has been the slowest to pass of my nearly seventeen years, yet the most exciting as well. I know Cyrus is almost of age to take a wife. My only course of action is to become a difficult merchant! I ask much more than I would have dared to dream in the past—but now I know my urgent need to build a dowry. Of course, I haven't asked Mordecai about this, but I see him counting his coins, always at night and in secret, and he never spends a penny on himself.

This, then, is the curse of love: that every moment apart be as slow as the turning of the seasons, and every moment together as fleeting as a dream.

9

Twenty-first Day of the Month of Kheshvan
Sixth Year of the Reign of Xerxes
Year 3397 after Creation

Today was such a difficult day—it is a wonder my hands find the strength to spill out in ink all the details here! Shethana told me news that Cyrus's father was going to announce a betrothal. No one knew any of the details, and Cyrus did not come to the market with his mother as usual. I was afraid to breathe until I knew, and every transaction was more maddening than the last, because no one had much information. Of course, no one could guess what disaster this day would mean to me.

So I waited. I didn't have the strength to brush the flies away from our meats, but rather, my eyes darted from customer to customer, praying for news, praying for relief. When at last I saw Cyrus, his downcast expression made me turn cold in the Arab sun. He walked directly to my table. He never would have done that in the past, and I wondered what awful thing had changed now. He asked, in a too loud voice, the price of my lamb. I told him, and he silently handed over the money. As I turned to wrap his selection, my fingers stumbling over the twine, he whispered between us, "Meet me tonight on the mountain." Then he left.

A second earlier I had been praying for people to wander into my tent so I could get information; now I was willing them to get out so I could flee to Cyrus and learn of our fate. The hours passed, the sun mocking me as it refused to set, but at last the day was over. I folded my tent and waited until I was alone in the marketplace, then hid my tent behind a rock and dashed for the mountain.

I found Cyrus there, sitting and staring toward the palace. The setting sun made it sparkle like a golden treasure from the ark, but tonight it seemed garish and intrusive. I did not want any eyes on us, not even the dead eyes of gold and silver.

Cyrus looked strained as he turned to me. "My father has chosen a husband for my sister."

His words were lifeless, but oh, how they brought life to me at once! I couldn't help but smile and breathe a sigh of utter relief.

"Cyrus! I thought it was you who were betrothed. This day has been an endless torture for me!" I cried.

But Cyrus made no move to comfort me. "You don't understand, Esther. My sister has no affection for this man, but of course, they have not asked her. She loathes him. He is a member of the family of descendants of Agag,[1] a dreadful, wicked man."

---

1 The Jews and the Agagites were ancient enemies. The Jewish king Saul was ordered by God to kill King Agag and all his people in a battle, but Saul spared King Agag for a few days, with the intention of killing him later. During this interval, it is believed that King Agag impregnated a servant before he was finally killed by the prophet Samuel. Agag's kingdom had always been bent on exterminating the Jews; now a remnant would live on and continue the blood feud in the Middle East.

I understood at once and frowned. "But a wicked man with money."

Cyrus gave me my first smile of the night. "Yes, quite a lot of money. His father has political connections and is said to be friends with the prime minister to King Xerxes, and the prime minister is himself an Agagite. My father needs this connection, but he cannot afford it. The dowry for my sister will leave us very little to live on. I fear this may push our own love in an unwelcome direction."

Cyrus winced; I could not tell if he was angry for his sister, or sad for us, for he covered his eyes with his hand and rubbed at them with his finger and thumb.

"What shall we do, Cyrus?" I asked softly.

Cyrus looked at me now and found his strength. "We shall not waste our time. You must approach Mordecai about a dowry, and I will stall my father from selecting a bride for me until I can tell him what Mordecai might offer."

He leaned over to me and gently lifted a small flower from the rock he was sitting on. Smiling, he held it out to me and kissed me. His kisses were a welcome darkness that I could get lost in; nothing from the village seemed real or near. I could only feel his lips and his beating heart and pray my eyes would never open from this moment, but they did. Ah, but they always do, even when I am only dreaming. Now Cyrus nudged me to begin my climb back down.

"My sister's wedding is in a month. We can do nothing until then. See what you can find out, and meet me here on the eve of the first full moon." He blew me a kiss and I left.

10

Tenth Day of the Month of Kislev
Sixth Year of the Reign of Xerxes
Year 3397 after Creation

Mordecai has told me nothing. He is trying to do the right thing; how can he know how wrong it is making everything for me? It is not proper, he insists, for a girl to know the details of her dowry. A Hebrew's worth is not measured in gold, and we must not think of marriage as a transaction. It is a sacrament, a holy creation of G-d, he says, and the sordid talk of coins can only muddy what is holy. I am to go to market and return to the home and maintain myself in every respect with honor. It is not good that I am an orphan, and I must give the villagers no other reason to cast aspersions on me. Mordecai insists that I give no one a chance to wag their tongues, no matter how innocent the actions I take. If the village must place a worth on my head, let me not be the one to haggle down the price.

Mordecai, my old cousin! I do not think in that way, but I know my beloved's father does and so I obey carefully. I am at a total loss to know what to tell Cyrus. I have thought of sneaking into Mordecai's closet at night, while he sleeps, and counting the coins, but how could I ever do that without awakening him? I have tried feigning sleep while he counts, and lying in the darkness, I count each coin's sharp report as it lands in the money jar. And so I know the total number of coins, but not their value. Cyrus is going to be disappointed. I could lie, but the lie would be exposed on our wedding day, which would surely bring a curse on our house.

The first full moon should be in two days. I will go and tell the truth. I love Cyrus, so why can't I tell him everything exactly as it is? There is no place for deception in the marriage bed, so I will not offer myself to him that way. I must state the truth, present the situation clearly, and trust G-d to work the details out in the open. I bow each morning and eve toward Jerusalem, my fervent prayers begging for swift action even as I lie still, hands upturned to receive G-d's blessing.

II

Sixth Day of the Month of Tammuz
Sixth Year of the Reign of Xerxes
Year 3397 after Creation

How thankful am I that Mordecai is so involved in the Jewish underground. He is forever slipping away for secret meetings, discussing how best to remove ourselves from the empire and return to Jerusalem to continue work rebuilding the Temple. He is focused on keeping his own secrets, and it has blinded him to mine. Tonight I am going to sneak away after the market and meet Cyrus.

The wedding of his little sister was a triumph, Mordecai tells me ... a triumph of greed. He said that no one believed the girl felt anything but fear and mistrust for her groom. Not that it mattered. The groom was busy feeling the dowry bag, satisfied that all this money would come with a warm body for his bed as well. Cyrus's father measured the wine carefully; a few people got enough to get drunk, but they were the people from the groom's side, with much to lose by being weakened in the presence of this climber.

I know, dear diary, that this is not a family I would have chosen to marry into, that I do not sound very wise smiting in words the very house I will be pledged to uphold. But it is Cyrus I want, and I will choose to believe G-d will redeem his parents in time. The rabbi has told us that G-d uses people to refine us, to call forth our greater character. I am sure it will be thus with Cyrus's family. I will continue their line, but they will make my name great. Ha! It is so much fun to dream so, even as I watch the sun rise and know that soon, this very night, I will be in Cyrus's arms, and my future will take its first true steps toward fulfillment.

12

*Third Day of the Month of Elul
Sixth Year of the Reign of Xerxes
Year 3397 after Creation*

I heard a legend once that, in the great oceans, there are monsters beneath the calm of the waters that can reach up, grab a man, and carry him to his doom. As a girl, I loved these stories, for in the safety of our home, I knew I would never even see these waters, and no monster could find me in my bed.

I know now many things, many things I wish to forget. I know now there are monsters, and calm waters can boil with danger at any moment.

I don't know how to write everything of this evening, and in truth, I don't know who the monsters are in my tale. But let me try now.

Cyrus and I met on the mountain, and seeing him soothed the jagged edges of my spirit once more. The world always seems so cold until I feel the warmth of his hand. I told what I knew, which was not much, of course. I knew the number of coins but not their value. Cyrus told me his father had made no mention of selecting a bride, but that his father had spent more time with the Agagite men. (It makes me sad to think of Cyrus's father betraying the Jews by befriending those who had once sought to kill us. But there are some in our community who believe that this hatred of Jews is a thing long past, and that the best we can do is blend in with our culture, not to draw so many distinctions between the godless and our G-d.)

Queen Vashti, forever in exile, has produced an heir to the throne, Artaxerxes. What a cruel man Xerxes must be to cast her away when she was with his child. But the Agagite men have begun to form an alliance with Vashti, to supply her needs and care for the son, still yet an infant. He is of no threat to the throne—yet—but even now the baby is a powerful ally.

We talked of our plans, or rather, we talked of what plans we needed, and the fears that had settled into my bosom slowly evaporated. But then, as we turned to leave, a shrill scream sounded from just above us. I knew instinctively what my eyes would find when I turned. And there she was; the animal the Jewish men believed was vomited out of Hades before her gates were closed by G-d. She was undoubtedly the one who had killed so many of our flocks, and rumor had it she had taken a child from a village in the west. A mountain lion, her sick green eyes lit with anger and surveying us, intruders in her kingdom of death. Her muscles moved like churning sands as she stepped lower to us, growling and showing us her filthy fangs.

Cyrus made a move to push me behind, and that's when she jumped. Her powerful arm outstretched, she swiped at him and Cyrus stumbled and fell. He rolled downward, toward the edge of the rocks, and she was on top of him at once, her fangs ripping at his thick leather vest as he kicked at her and screamed. I could see she was trying to lunge in toward his neck. G-d must have been on the mountain, too, because I found myself tearing into Cyrus's bag lying on the ground near our meeting place. Inside was his knife, the knife the elders gave to him on the hunt for his thirteenth birthday. It had been sufficient to skin a rabbit, but what could it do here?

I plunged the knife into the cat, sinking it up to its small hilt. The cat screamed and turned toward me, the knife still embedded in her side. She panted heavily as she edged closer. I could see Cyrus was bleeding from a gash in his chest, but he moved to his feet and grabbed a rock, swinging it at her from behind, bringing it down on her head. The great cat lost her footing and was disoriented, but only for a moment. Her head swung slowly back to Cyrus, and the curtain of her lips revealed their terrible drama, the fangs now whetted for the kill.

There was no more time. I shoved my outstretched arms into her side. She stumbled toward the ledge but regained her footing, and with a low hissing growl continued to creep toward Cyrus for her kill. I took a desperate breath, and this time, shoved with all my might. Her back leg went off the ledge and she hissed at me, too, but it was too late. Cyrus slammed his rock against her leg closest to him, and she jerked it away, snarling. Her footing gone now, she slipped over the edge and fell, hitting larger rocks and turning, end over end, until she at last righted herself and glared back up the mountain toward us. Her eyes were alive with an evil fire, but she moved now into the shadows and disappeared.

I ran to Cyrus and helped him to his feet.

"You saved my life," he said.

I think he looked at me with suspicion. But why would it be strange that a girl can thrust a knife, or find the strength to face an enemy? Even my dear Cyrus has these strange ideas of what a woman is capable of. Or perhaps I am the strange one, not to limit myself there.

But we came slowly down the mountain. Cyrus's wound was not as bad as I might have feared, but this was not what was draining the blood from his heart, or mine. He was not strong enough to walk home alone, nor could I leave him at the foot of the mountain. We would have to go together for help, and what story could we give to cover our deception?

Instinctively, our feet shuffled in unison toward the home of the village healer. She was a kind but withered old woman, long since entrusted with the most precious secrets of our people, and many years skilled in the art of healing. Even the Egyptians came to her when their magicians failed them. It did not surprise us that she opened her door before we were close enough to knock.

I eased Cyrus into the chair, and the woman kept her back to us as she poured honey into a bowl and beat against it a thick switch of rosemary and another herb I did not recognize. She spoke as she worked, her home lit by a single fat wax candle perched on her small table.

"The night wind told me the great cat was near. How is it your young ears did not hear it too?" she asked.

We could not answer her.

"Why were you out of your beds at this hour?" she asked softly.

Cyrus spoke first. "Esther met me tonight on the mountain to plan our betrothal. My father will choose another bride unless

I can act first. Esther was there against her good judgment, at my pleading."

The old woman looked at me, then at Cyrus, studying his wounds, and my condition. "It looks as if Esther's judgment is good indeed. How did you outsmart the beast, Esther?" She dipped a cloth in a basin of water and wiped gently at Cyrus's wounds, cleansing them from the pebbles and grass sticking to the clotting blood. Cyrus tried not to wince, then kept his eyes closed.

I told the healer what had happened and she nodded. "The cat is pregnant, and is becoming unsteady on her feet. Your instincts guided you well," she said.

The honey was applied next and then a clean cloth wrapped several times around his chest to hold the cure against him tightly. She walked to her window and held her head up to the stars. She seemed to be tasting the night air.

She turned to us. "I have heard the talk in the village. Cyrus's father has indeed chosen another bride, and he has not made his plans known. But your dilemma is now doubled, for Cyrus must rest here tonight until his bleeding has stopped. I will return with his father in a little while, and how will you two explain this misadventure tonight, without lying? Think carefully of what you will say. As for you"—and here she faced me—"Mordecai is meeting with the elders once more, and their candles burn low. You will be able to keep your deception from him at least for tonight."

Cyrus seemed so weak and tired. I could not leave him as the healer went to find his father. There was so much to explain that we had little to say to each other. Cyrus's father soon entered the small doorway and stood staring at us. He didn't seem concerned for Cyrus, but perhaps the old woman had given him many details already.

"What has happened?" he demanded.

Cyrus began to explain about the cat, but his father interrupted. "Your wounds tell the story plainly enough. I want to know about this girl."

Cyrus began. I was never so scared, and so proud, as hearing Cyrus explain his feelings for me, and his plan for us to be married after Mordecai raised a significant dowry.

"Is that what this is about?" his father asked. His tone changed from angry to calm, but somehow I was still frightened. "You think I need this dowry for you to be together? Nonsense. We have plenty of money without begging for it from your wife. But I must tell you, I am surprised at this revelation. I had intended to arrange a marriage to a girl from another village, the daughter of an Egyptian financier in the market. She's quite stunning."

Cyrus and I exchanged looks, and Cyrus shook his head at his father.

"Well, then, the matter is settled." Cyrus's father smiled at us both. "Let us go about our business now as usual, children. Your secret will be safe with me. I only ask for time, and your trust. I will work out the details with Mordecai, but in my own way. We must not make him feel ashamed at so little a dowry. If you give me time, I will give him his dignity, and you, your marriage."

I rose and kissed him on the cheek. He grabbed my arm and looked at me closely, his breath hot on my cheek. There was something about his hands on my arm, as if I could feel them moving all over, although in truth they didn't move their grip. I didn't like it.

"You are indeed a beautiful girl," he said. "Any man would be fortunate to call you his own."

I left and ran through the dark streets to my home, making sure I was in bed and feigning sleep before Mordecai returned.

13

Third Day of the Month of Tevet
Seventh Year of the Reign of Xerxes
Year 3398 after Creation

The hellcat is long gone from our village, seeking new victims to devour. The women are still wearing their amulets and cursing the demons, but they do not know what it was that stalked the village at night. Their superstitious talk kept the market lively for weeks, but it grew quiet until a new, darker shadow showed itself.

Rumors have gone into the village ahead of the king's men. Xerxes will take a bride from among his people! Girls have begun feverishly preparing for the selection day, as if they can ripen themselves into choice fruit in mere days. But in my quiet household, as Mordecai prepares for a meeting with the Jewish elders, dread coils around my heart. My stomach tightens at every mention of the coming selection. *Surely the Jews will be exempt,* I silently plead to no one. The elders believe my people will not be highly favored during the choosing, but neither should we interfere with the king's will. Our exile is dishonorable to the Persians, and that doesn't commend a girl. The palace will avoid taking a Jew.

But my mind leaps forward to the moment the men will wander through our village. When their eyes rove over every girl, will they stop to rest on me? I know Cyrus will find a way to ransom me from that day. I have resolved to trust G-d in the matters of my heart, and so I pray for Cyrus's father, for his heart to be turned back toward his people, and opened to his son's love for this girl. I pray he keeps his promise to me, and soon.

But the selection day is drawing near. Each morning this week has found me still in my bed, my heart filled with a fear as yellow and curdled as the eggs in the market. Although Mordecai has assured me that I will not be chosen, I have heard the rumors stealing through the village. If a girl is chosen, she will be taken away to the king's palace, never to return again. The king has issued a decree that the chosen ones will spend a year preparing for one night with him; and after that, they will become his wives, and live in his palace for the remainder of their days … or the remainder of his reign, whichever ends first. The king surely gives deadly wedding gifts; for every girl knows she will die with the king. Many kings, and their nobles, do not die a natural cause.

Lord, you allowed my parents to be taken from me, and I have made my peace with that. Will you allow my new life with Cyrus to be stolen as well? You delivered me from dire and desperate grief and placed me here. I know it was Your hand that brought me here, that has given me shelter and comfort and healing. You would not now open the wound again, and abandon me to heartache once more! The meager hopes I have are enough to sustain me; I would not care for the palace if the palace was forced upon me.

Yet I know I am the only girl in our village who fears the selection so. The other girls see only the relief from toil in the desert sun, to be brought to a palace of luxury and indulgence, to be transformed from their humble lives into the existence of the royal ones. It is a dream too sweet to wake from, they say.

14

Nineteenth Day of the Month of Tevet
Seventh Year of the Reign of Xerxes
Year 3398 after Creation

I saw Cyrus in the market today, and I couldn't help it. I waved him over to my booth. I knew his mother would not approve of such behavior, but I feel desperate for news, for assurances. Cyrus made the usual motions as if he was surveying my goods, but he whispered to me exactly what I needed to hear. His father has been making many plans, he says, and there is no need to worry.

"He tells me there will be a wonderful future for us both and we must trust him. All will be revealed at the right moment, he says." Cyrus sounded confident.

I felt at ease once more. "The selection day is drawing so near, Cyrus," I told him, as I wrapped a small dried steak and handed it to him. "But I will not be afraid if you tell me not to."

Cyrus took the steak and looked at me with a seriousness that made me love him all over again. "Do not be afraid. I, Cyrus, pledge to you that we will not be separated by this pagan king seeking women for his harem. Nothing can take you from me. We will be together."

And he left. I did feel better, for hours perhaps, but am afraid again now, as I write this, and can see candles burning late, as mothers prepare their daughters. My faith is such a strange thing—that it can stay strong at such moments, yet must be buoyed up again so frequently.

15

Nineteenth Day of the Month of Tevet
Seventh Year of the Reign of Xerxes
Year 3398 after Creation

I wish now I had recorded so much more of home. Yet I began this diary just before I turned sixteen, and I did not suspect my years there would be brief. I am only seventeen, but already the time of my youth has slipped through my fingers while I grasped this pen to record my petty thoughts. If only I had known what this day would bring.

This morning I heard the horses stomping through the village, their snorts as heavy and urgent as a trumpet call. I peeked out my window just in time to see a father step out of his home, presenting his daughter for inspection. The commissioner, the man appointed from Susa by the king to choose the women, surveyed her slowly. This was the look I knew from the market, when a buyer is not sure of either the goods or the price, and the seller must offer some enticement.

At her father's command, the girl loosened her robe so the men could more clearly see her form. She never lifted her eyes from the sandy road as they ordered her into the caravan. She did not say good-bye. The commissioner nodded to a palace guard, who placed something in the father's hand. He walked to his home, looking satisfied, feeling the weight in his palm. I understood now why our village embraced the selection day. They received a bride price without giving a dowry and were freed of one mouth to feed.

Now I heard Mordecai moving about quickly in the front room. He swept the money from the market across the table, giving our meager coins the appearance of many, and fetched his market ledger. He saw my look of fear and motioned for me to hide in the next room. I did. And then I heard the voice.

"Bring out your daughter." It was a command.

"I have no daughter," was Mordecai's indifferent reply. I heard the coins clinking against each other.

What an odd time to count them, I thought.

"She is not his daughter, indeed, but a cousin!" This new voice was insistent and spiteful, and I knew it at once. It was Cyrus's father.

So this was his plan! The father's reply to our love was clever, and clear. Remove me from the village so Cyrus will choose the more suitable wife. A wife who will bring more than just her heart to the marriage bed.

The palace guard entreated Mordecai again: "Bring us your cousin, my friend. Have you not heard that the king desires a new queen?"

Mordecai's voice remained unchanged. "This girl is not to the king's liking."

Cyrus's father spoke in a rush of words. "She is the most beautiful girl in the village! My boy talks of nothing else! Her eyes are the color of the flowers that bloom at night along the city wall! Her hair is spun silk from the East! You must see her."

"Out!" Mordecai spoke sharply now, ordering Cyrus's father

to leave. Then his voice grew low as he spoke alone to the guard. "Perhaps if I were to go into this next room to console my cousin on the misfortune of being rejected, you could find something here of worth to take to the king on our behalf. Or you could use it to sweeten your own journey."

I understood now why Mordecai had chosen this moment to count our money from the market.

I heard no reply. The guard stepped into the room I was in and held out his hand. Seeing him in my bedroom, his armor and sword reflecting the breakfast sun, was a nightmare I could not shake myself from. I was led, past Mordecai, to the entrance of our home, where several men stood with scrolls. The commissioner, who was riding a horse, judged me from his perch. A knowing glance passed between him and the guard, then the men began to write.

I had been chosen.

Mordecai looked stricken as the guards pointed me to the caravan. He ran to embrace me, and as he covered my face with his tears, he gave me a warning: "Tell no one you are a Jew. The tides may soon turn for our people here, and I do not want you caught in the current." Then he pushed two scrolls into my hands, which I hid in my robe.

The guards pried me loose and forced me into the caravan. My last glimpse was of Mordecai, weeping, in front of my home. He did not reach out for the money they offered. "Take it, Mordecai," I called to him, "for we do not know what lies ahead."

When Mordecai would not reach out his hand, the guards threw the money at his feet and turned toward another home. His eyes never left mine as I was led away. I was vaguely aware of the sounds of mothers weeping and fathers counting their coins as more and more girls were rounded up. The veil was brought down once more over the caravan, and I lost sight of Mordecai, and my home, forever.

Inside the caravan, a few girls talked merrily, their words as fast and free as the pleasures they described awaiting us. I did not believe much of what they said. Some girls simply stared ahead. Other girls, who had obviously gone unwillingly, were bound and thrown in the back of the group.

A very young girl, perhaps about eleven or twelve years old, was crying, cramped into a little corner of the caravan. I sought her out, putting my arms gently around her. She clung to me, crying out for her mother. I understood too well. Once I, too, had wept like this, separated forever from my own mother when she died. There were no sheltering arms that day for me; it had been weeks before Mordecai heard of the disaster and came to find me.

I held this girl tightly, letting her tears wet my dress. I knew what it was to weep alone for a mother. "What is your name?" I whispered to her.

"Yoshtya," was her reply, and my expression must have told her I had not heard the name before. She stopped her tears long enough to explain she was named after her people's god, a great spirit who had saved the world by answering the ninety-nine questions a demon posed. This demon would have destroyed all if it were not for the wisdom of her namesake. I patted her hand and she rested her head against me. I could not help but resent her god. How easy to escape with ninety-nine questions. I saw many more ahead.[1]

---

1 Read an excerpt from a speech by President George W. Bush to the United Nations in the appendix, page 276.

16

Twenty-second Day of the Month of Tevet
Seventh Year in the Reign of Xerxes
Year 3398 after Creation

We arrived at dusk at the gates of the king's gardens and were joined by another caravan coming to Susa from Persepolis.[1] Our caravan made a slow curve toward a palace nestled around the towering eden. Smells of jasmine and nectars, unearthly, intoxicating, came through the veils in greeting. We had been transported to a new world, and a new restlessness swept through the girls.

The caravan creaked to a halt, and low voices were heard just outside. The veil covering of the caravan was pulled away.

What we saw left us all breathless.

This palace was more splendid than I had dared to imagine even of heaven. The moon illuminated the soft glow of gold

---

1 While Susa, Esther's village, was the administrative capitol where Xerxes and his court spent their winters, Persepolis was the grand social and spiritual center. Persepolis, built by Xerxes' father, Darius, housed a harem, the king's palace, a treasury, and the greatest wonders of the ancient world, The Gate of All Nations and the Throne Hall. Persepolis was the favorite spring and autumn home of the king. Both cities are located in what is now modern-day Iran.

everywhere—the couches lounging underneath lazy trees, the urns and statues of the Persian gods, the columns along the massive entrance. The ambition that burned in the girls' eyes shone brighter. I could almost see a few of them trying on the queen's crown in their minds.

There was an inscription along the main entrance of the harem. The first portion was easy to read from where I stood:

> *A great god is Ahura Mazda,*[2]
> *who created this most excellent place,*
> *who created happiness for man,*
> *who set wisdom and capability down upon King*
> *Xerxes.*
> *Enter and be blessed.*

I wanted at this moment only to have Mordecai near, to see his own face taking this all in. It was too much for me to believe, and see, alone.

A warm hand found mine. My young traveling companion had stopped weeping now and was as overwhelmed as I. New guards whom we had not seen before approached the caravan. They had armor I had never seen, shields as big as my bed, and spears that could have run a bull through. One by one these guards led the girls out and down the path to the courtyard of the palace. The guards began assembling us according to province. Several other caravans

2 Ahura Mazda was a pagan deity worshipped in the empire, and closely tied to the early religion of Zoroastrianism. It is unclear whether Xerxes was a true Zoroastian, although he made use of many of the religion's teachings and beliefs in his public works and rulings.

had recently unloaded. We could see those girls peering from inside the palace, or moving inside as they cast backward glances to see us. Many of the girls, I could see, carried heavy bags of clothes, perfumes, and adornments. Many had brought their household gods with them. It was clear that they would not waste this opportunity. I wondered what it must have been like to have a mother prepare you for this moment. I wondered about my own mother. Would she have fixed my hair and patted my cheek as we waited for the guards that day, or would she have seen to it that my marriage to Cyrus was secured quickly? I swallowed back my envy and sadness as the guards showed me to my place in line.

Hours had passed since I had been stolen from my home. Cyrus must know by now. What had he done when he heard? In my mind I placed him coming over the wall, rescuing me at once. I lifted my robe at the edges so I could run at any moment. I willed myself to take in all these sights so that I might tell them to our children one day, the sole glance I had of the mad palace before Cyrus returned and I was safe again. I had saved him on the mountain; he would do no less for me here.

I was placed between two girls who had come well prepared. Their hair was coiled on the tops of their heads, their breath smelled of cloves, and even in the moonlight I could tell they had been carefully attended to that morning; their skin shone with oils underneath their lucent garments. I could also feel the girls' eyes taking me in and snickering. My heartbroken friend from the caravan, Yoshtya, was several rows in front of me, and she turned to meet my eyes. She had a mother, but a poor one. The girls were laughing at her, too. I tried to give her a smile.

The girl on my left spoke first: "What were you doing when you were called?"

It sounded more like a joke than a question.

The second girl spoke. "It's clear she wasn't at her grooming table!"

They stifled their giggles.

I heard many other girls talking too.

"Where are you from?"

"Did your family get a good bride price?"

"What have you brought?"

"Will the king choose tonight?"

As the stories circulated, and the boasting grew louder, the girls on either side of me seemed more aggrieved to be standing next to such an unadorned offering.

Finally one could hold her tongue no more: "This one didn't even bathe or dress for today! She thinks the king wants a shrew for a wife!" Her words were loud and cold.

"I am hoping to be sent home. I clearly do not belong here with you," I replied carefully.

Several girls rolled their eyes as they laughed, catching the attention of the guards, who drew nearer.

Then he appeared from inside the palace.

His limbs were dark, like the dark pines of the mountains. He moved with the grace of the sea, clothed in magnificent robes with sashes of linen and rings of gold. And his face—not unlike, perhaps, the faces I had seen in the market, but strangely radiant, as if his great wealth resided in his heart and not just in this palace. As he took a step down into the courtyard, I fell to my knees in humble respect. Never had I seen such a man or such a place. Perhaps I would still be returned home, but I prayed suddenly now to find favor and live in peace, even from afar, with this great man. I prayed he would forgive easily. I was not prepared. I was not as these other beauties in his presence.

I could hear the girls on either side of me stifling another giggle. I clenched my eyes shut. Had the king spied my shabby robe and loose hair?

Heavy, sure footsteps quieted the noise. "Why do you laugh?" A deep voice slid quietly between us.

The girl on my left answered first. "She thinks you are the king." Several girls laughed out loud. My heart raced as confusion rose to meet my fear, but I could not look up.

"And why should I not be?" His reply stung the girls into silence.

I felt a hand on my shoulder and found the courage to look up. "I am sorry," I stammered, feeling my nervous words tumble out now. "I've never ... I thought you were the king." I swallowed once. "Please be honored by my mistake and forgive your servant."

He smiled easily. "I am Hagai, and in charge of this harem palace. What is your name, child?"

"I am called Esther."

Hagai studied me, and again I grew afraid. "Why have you come in these clothes? Why did you make no attempt to please the king?" he asked.

"I should not have been chosen," I answered. "I am only an orphan who tends lambs and roses and sells my goods in the market. I am not wanted as a bride in my own village; how then could I be chosen by the king?" My heart was raw, hearing this truth aloud. If the girls had reason to laugh before, now their torment would be endless. It would be foolish to tell anyone of Cyrus, to alert them for the one surely coming soon.

Hagai took my hands in his, turning them over. My palms bore the evidence of carrying the rough wooden pails for miles every day, and from grinding my wheat and barley into flour to cook over the hot stones. Next, he ran his fingers through my hair, rubbing sections of it between two fingers. He traced the outline of my face, turning my cheeks in each direction with his wrist. Then he leaned forward to speak privately. "Have you any defects, child?"

I shook my head no.

"Have you ever sold yourself to a man?"

My eyebrows shot up in surprise; that was answer enough for him. He looked at my robe's bosom now, and as I grew afraid and my cheeks again flushed with shame, he lifted out the scrolls I had hidden.

"What are these?" he asked. "Surely an orphan cannot read or write."

"But I can, gracious lord!" I replied in earnest, for I did not want him to keep the scrolls. "I was taken in by a cousin, and he has spent long hours teaching me this art. It has brought me consolation on many nights, and with your permission, lord, it will again be my comfort." I tentatively held out my hand to him.

He spun on his heel and barked a command: "Take her to the Chamber of Pearls. Assign Ashtari to her, and six more of our best handmaidens." He turned once more to me and smiled. "Let us see the flower that will bloom under our care." And, placing the scrolls back inside my robes, he nudged me toward the guards who were coming to escort me.

Hagai turned now to address all the girls assembled. "You have been brought tonight to the harem of the great King Xerxes. My name is Hagai, and I am your father now, your one source of sustenance and advancement." (Here he eyed the taunting girls plainly.) "Tomorrow will mark your first day in this new world. You will each be given one year of beauty treatments: six months of cleansing and softening of the skin, and six months of cosmetics and adornments. At the end of your time here, you will be led to King Xerxes for his good pleasure. You will take only what you have learned here, plus one gift to offer for his good graces, and you will have only one night to please him. One of you will, perhaps, be chosen as the new queen to rule over us all. I bid you to think on these things, and as my servants escort you to your chambers, I bid you good night."

I was led, stunned, past all the girls, up the marble stairs into the harem palace. As I passed my little traveling companion, she smiled broadly at me. My knees grew weaker with every step, for deeper inside the harem were more riches. Now I knew why the outside world had seemed so poor: Surely everything of wealth had been brought here. I was accustomed to walking barefoot over the hot-caked sand to fetch our water; here every step was greeted by a cool mosaic of precious stones and pearls, and water flowed from a waterfall large enough to bathe in. Several girls lounged in its mists as servants stood close by, fanning them. Wild thoughts surged through my head. I wanted to scrape up the floor and run out there. Mordecai and I could be free with the riches of just the floor. Mordecai could buy a wife, and I would have a dowry.

"Ashtari!" my guide called out. "Your newest one has arrived!"

As we wound up a marble staircase that seemed to ascend to heaven itself, a silk curtain parted slowly and the most beautiful woman I had ever seen glided out to meet us. Her hair was wrapped in precious jewels that seemed to cascade down her body, resting on her neck, fingers, waist, and even her toes. Her lips were rouged to a smoky red and a stroke of black kohl gave her the gaze of a tiger. She smiled softly at me and dismissed the guard.

Silently, she led me inside by the hand and motioned for me to sit. The couch she gestured to was gold, with bull heads carved on each end, scarlet linen pillows tied with blue cords, and bells along the edge of the covering that made a soft music when I sat. The floor seemed to be made out of one endless pearl, little arcs of color washing across it as the light from a hole in the ceiling filtered down. There were hanging plants of all kinds, some with fruits and some with small flowers dripping with nectar. There was a bed covered in tapestries and gold basins filled with water and floating blossoms. Along the back wall were jeweled jars of all types and fashions. The staircase that led up to this room continued on past us to somewhere overhead.

"My name is Ashtari. You will be served by me, and the six maids I have chosen. While you remain in this harem, you are under my care. Until you understand our world here, I would ask you to give yourself over to my counsel completely. Do not talk to anyone other than your servants and Hagai." She looked over the balcony toward the floor of the harem. "There are women down there who have set themselves against you."

"Me?" I asked.

Ashtari smiled. "Let us begin."

She clapped her hands and six women appeared from just beyond a silk curtain across the room. They nodded at me with careful smiles and stood behind Ashtari, who took a seat on a gilded chair with crystal feet, neatly tucking her feet under her body.

She motioned me to the room's center. "Please disrobe."

They all stood there, staring. Blood rushed to my face. I stood for a moment, hoping I had not heard this command correctly. But Ashtari's cool gaze, and that of the waiting servants, told me I must obey. My hands found the fastened cord on my worn garments, and I began to remove my robes. (My clothes were soiled, yet had been so serviceable for the lambs and hot fires at home. I could not be glad for them now.) I felt only shame, standing bare before these creatures of comfort and elegance.

"Turn please," Ashtari commanded gently. I could hear them whispering, one to another, and Ashtari giving careful directions. Oh, the whispers in this place! Suddenly I wanted nothing more than to turn and run home. For there, although nothing was mine, I was free. Here, wealth was all around me, but I was a prisoner.

When I had spun slowly for their inspection, the smallest hand-maiden took me by the hand and led me, still bare, up the stairs. I felt the eyes of the girls on the main harem floor below. I was so grateful to be unable to hear their whispers, too. They hated me already, and here I was, naked before their stabbing eyes. As I climbed, away from the harem and the whispers and vengeful glances, I could see now that the stairs opened to the roof of the harem. The roof was itself a garden, with a large pool to one side. The girls motioned me in, and to sit, and began pouring the water over my hair and shoulders, squeezing fruits and their juices into my hair and rubbing the scent in vigorously. With a porous stone they rubbed at the rough skin of my hands and feet. I took a deep breath now, and let the water do its healing work on my exhausted body. My mind was scattered in so many directions, I did not even try to pull in the pieces. I longed to be alone and to sleep this nightmare away.

Ashtari came and stood by the side of the bath. "After the girls dress you, they will return you to your quarters. You will be fed, and then sleep. Tomorrow our work must begin in earnest." (And it happened as she said. Perhaps everything here does—I will have to learn more about my exotic jailer.)

But I was washed and, mercifully, robed, and led back down to my chambers. A low table had been brought in, and although there were steaming dishes set forth, I could not tell what was inside. I sank into a floor cushion and a girl came forward to serve me. I motioned her away.

"I know how to eat," I told her.

She looked confused.

"Should you join me?" I asked.

Now she looked stricken. "I am to serve you," she insisted.

When I shook my head no and began lifting the lid from the dishes, she huffed in exasperation and fled downstairs. I was, at last, alone, even if I would have to explain my behavior to Ashtari later. Hunger tore at my stomach, and the relief of being alone and this dreadful day being done made me giddy at the prospect of being left alone with a platter of the king's fare.

I lifted the lid on the deep, etched silver bowl. My nose recoiled before my mind could decipher the smell. The soup was a thick green sludge, with waxy fat beans floating like dead fish in the river, and an odor to match. I closed the lid. The next dish proved happier, for it was rice. This rice had a new sort of spice sprinkled on it, but it was soft, and palatable, and familiar. The largest dish I saved for last—a tremendous gold plate, with foreign writing all along the edges, covered by a dome of gold inlaid with a band of silver. I stared at it a moment, deciding if it held friend or foe, and lifted the lid. It was a shank of lamb, rubbed with spices and roasted with lemons and onions. How could something make me so happy and so forlorn at the same time? Lamb was what I sold in the market, for feasts and celebrations, and here I was, alone, a prisoner whose very cell was coveted by hundreds of girls. I had never tasted lamb, the price even of my own being too dear. Mordecai and I had eaten only goat and fish. "G-d bless the hands that prepared this dish," I whispered, "and forgive me for eating it." It was delicious. I mashed the tomatoes into the rice, and gnawed at the lamb bone. I would not think of home tonight. I could not and still keep my appetite. I had but a moment's strength from the service of the girls and my warm bath. To think of home, of Cyrus, would leave me too weak to think of an escape.

I looked round the room once more, my eyes no longer shy. Along the wall that held the jeweled jars was a mural etched in gold, with a braid of bronze running along the bottom. The mural told the story of the ancient kings who had held sway over this palace. Their dead eyes watched me eat. Who was this king who now controlled all of this wealth? Why did he want so many girls? My people married once, for life. What could this king want with each of us that he could not find in one woman?

A noise behind me caught my ear, and I turned to see Ashtari coming up the stairs. She carried a small platter of steaming tea, with fruits and what looked like bits of hardened honey. Another servant, the one who had grown so aggrieved with my behavior at dinner, followed behind her. The servant cast a hopeless glance at me as she cleared my table and left. Ashtari sat opposite me, with her tray between us. Silently, she poured us each a cup of tea. I accepted mine. She held my gaze as she put one of the hardened bits of honey into her mouth, holding it between her teeth as she sipped a long draught of the hot tea. I did the same. It was indeed like honey, only sweeter. The bitter tea drawn through it became like a tonic to me. Once again, I found my shoulders dropping and deep breaths finding their way out of my lungs.

"Is it what you expected?" Ashtari broke the silence between us.

"Nothing is what I expected. I wanted only to remain at home. How is it a life can change from one sunset to the next, in such terrible, unforeseen ways?" I could not reveal myself as a Jew, or as a girl already pledged in love, but I would not hide the truth.

Ashtari's expression did not change. "You are not the first to be brought here unhappy, and you will not be the last. It is not for us to choose our days."

We sipped our tea in silence then.

Below us I could see girls moving about, as I peered through the ornate ledge near the staircase. The girls were of all nations, and beautiful beyond description. Some wore such immodest outfits! Only mere belts of coins that held loosely draped fabric over their most secret places, and thin scarves covering their breasts as well. Some wore thickly woven brocaded jackets and flowing black pants that shimmered against the jeweled floor. Some wore their hair loose; others had it sculpted in the most marvelous ways on top of their heads. But one woman, moving slowly through them, surely ruled them all. Alongside her walked a white tiger, held to her by a heavy gold chain. She was a dark beauty with straight black hair falling to her waist and a robe of white cinched at her waist with another gold rope. Other girls moved quickly out of her way. As if she could feel my eyes, this woman stopped and stared toward me in my haven above them all. She glared at me and made a series of small, delicate signs with her hands. I didn't think they were good.

Ashtari caught my expression and looked over the ledge. She hissed something in another tongue I did not recognize to this woman, who continued her walk to another room in the palace.

"That was Yoon-Mai. Do not let her disturb you, but do not cross her path if you can help it while you are here. She is favored to be the new queen, and she has a taste for blood." Ashtari related this all in a calm voice, but I felt more uncertain with every word.

As Ashtari stood to leave me, I found the courage to ask the question that had been itching at the back of my mind for several minutes. "Ashtari, if the king is looking for a beautiful girl from this harem to become queen, why have you not gone into him yourself?"

Her gaze became cool, and her eyes swept the room for servants. Seeing none, she leaned closer and, her gaze still even with mine, lifted her skirt to one side. My stomach lurched, and I forced myself to meet her eyes once more. The flesh over her right thigh was purple and spoiled, dark scars shooting like sunbursts from the edge of the wound. Satisfied that I had seen my answer, she lowered her skirt and explained.

"When I was a young girl, I lived with my family along the banks of the Nile. One day when I had gone to the river to fetch some water, I stepped near a cobra. When I saw its hood, I screamed and startled the river animals. One animal fleeing the water trampled it, but the cobra still was able to strike my thigh before it died. My parents called on a healer, a Jew, and he worked many days to save me. He succeeded, but my parents could not pay his fee. He insisted on receiving the money immediately. He said he had to make a holy pilgrimage. It was time for the Jewish sacrifices, he said. My parents begged him to wait another week, until our harvest came in, but he refused. My parents sold me to the king's service to pay the healer's fees. So I was spared, but lost forever to them. I do not know why the Jews are tolerated in this land."

Ashtari was looking off the balcony now toward the horizon, and I wondered if she was seeing her family in her mind's eye. She turned and smiled. "Hagai has made me the highest ranking servant in his care, for only a truly beautiful woman knows how to find the beauty in another. And I see he has again chosen exceptionally well, for you are indeed more lovely than the others." She leaned closer. "We all heard rumors of a girl in the village who was more beautiful than Vashti, though none of us dared to dream it."

I blushed, feeling betrayed that this beauty she saw in me dared to take me places I would have resisted.

"But there will be many days for stories," Ashtari said. "Mine has ended, and tomorrow yours begins in earnest."[3]

---

3 See corresponding commentary in the appendix, page 278.

17

*Thirtieth Day of the Month of Tevet
Seventh Year of the Reign of Xerxes
Year 3398 after Creation*

Niloufar is her name. She told me when she woke me in the morning, sitting on my bed and draping warm cloths over my eyes,
swollen from crying myself to sleep. Niloufar is the servant I scorned
by refusing her service at dinner last night. Clearly she is a girl who
loves to serve, and she doted on me as a mother might have, except
that Niloufar is several years younger than I am. I wondered if I had
said anything in my sleep; if she had been near to hear his name from
my lips.

"Ashtari is waiting for you upstairs, in the garden bath," she said
softly.

In a moment between cloths, I tried to rub my eyes with the
back of my hands, but Niloufar grabbed them quickly. "You must
not stretch the skin around your eyes!" she admonished me. From her
expression, I understood that she was surprised at my clumsy error.

"Niloufar," I sighed, "my people are not so concerned with these
things. You will have to give me time to adjust to your ways."

Niloufar studied me for a moment, then glanced at my scrolls lying on the table nearest my bed. Only my diary was left about in plain view; the other, the scroll written in Mordecai's hand, was safely hidden until I knew the right time had come to read it. He had shoved two scrolls to me as I was taken. On the caravan I discovered one was a letter from him, and I waited to be truly alone before I opened it. The right time had not yet come, as these servants and girls swirled all around me with their endless list of chores: baths, hair, and meals. And now I knew even my sleep would be attended to, lest I undid their magic around my eyes.

"You are the one who reads and writes?" she asked.

I nodded and pressed the warm cloths against my eyes once more. I could hear her picking up the scroll to look at it. I wasn't worried she would read it, for I already had guessed from her tone that she couldn't.

"You are too pale to be Egyptian. This is an Egyptian scroll." She sat, waiting for an explanation, although already I knew from her demeanor that she had no rank here to request one.

"No, Niloufar, I am not Egyptian, although I write on scrolls much like what the Egyptians use. That is because animal skins as the Greeks use are too precious in my village, and the clay tablets others use are deemed for more important matters than a girl's quiet thoughts."

Niloufar seemed satisfied with the answer. She picked up a sea sponge and large robe and led me upstairs for another bath.

Now it was my turn to ask a curious question. "Who carries the water up to the roof, Niloufar? It must be a terrible chore."

Niloufar again rolled her eyes at me. I could tell her patience with my ignorance would not last. "Whoever heard of carrying water? The water here flows from the mountains. Channels were cut, aqueducts they are called, and they carry fresh water to the palaces." Niloufar was glad to give me this information because it meant she could barrage me with more questions of her own.

"If you write," she asked, "you must also be allowed to read, perhaps even books? I have heard that a Greek has penned a story called *The Odyssey*. It's a bit old now, but I hear it is still quite entertaining. Have you been allowed to read it? You could recite passages to the servants."

I shook my head that I had not read it.

"You must give me details about your life and your people. I have lived in this harem since I was weaned," Niloufar implored, disappointed that I would not be a source of amusement.

I stopped for a moment on the stairs. What could I tell her? "My people live here in Susa." I finally answered and resumed our ascent.

"But Susa is the capital! How can your people not know the practices of the land?"

I did not have time to reply, mercifully, as we emerged into the morning sun. Ashtari waved Niloufar away, who was still staring suspiciously at me. Ashtari motioned me to stand before a basin. A man stood close by with a razor. Another woman hovered near him, armed with a slender thread she held between her teeth and the fingers of one hand.

"Do you prefer to shave your head, or keep your hair?" she asked.

"No!" I gasped, involuntarily grasping the ends of my hair.

Ashtari and the man laughed. Then she lifted her hair entirely off her head—she was bald!

"It's a wig, Esther. My people wear wigs and keep their heads shaved cleanly. But I see that I will not convert you to this custom. We will, however, begin your preparation for the king by removing all other hair. You are to be stripped completely clean of hair, save for your head, and then washed once more. Our first few months together will consist only of preparing your body to receive the king's touch. You will bathe daily and be rubbed down each morning and eve with oil of myrrh. You are to eat the portions set before you without question, for your body is to be rounded out. Only after you have been softened and conditioned will you begin learning the arts of seduction and presentation. For now, Niloufar will stay to escort you back to your chambers and there we will begin to attend to your diet."

Ashtari circled me slowly, pointing to my arms and legs, and giving commands to one of the eunuchs.

"You are too thin to be brought to the king, you know. No man wants to reach for a woman and find only bones," she told me. "You must eat everything set before you, Esther. Even the soup."

She gave me a smile and motioned now for servants to step forward and begin the process of removing all hair. They worked, oblivious to my cries of pain and protest. They removed hairs I had never contemplated; surely they would not be a bother to a king who would only know me for one night? But nothing was spared attention; to my horror, even the sacred places were stripped clean.

I looked back and forth between Ashtari and her servants. I could not believe this was happening.

But it was.

18

Second Day of the Month of Shevat
Seventh Year of the Reign of Xerxes
Year 3398 after Creation

I do not know how long I will be here, nor if I will be able to get more scroll as I need it. Once again, I am forced to reserve this precious scroll. I am the only one among these girls who reads and writes; all think it a waste of my precious year here to record my thoughts. But I am alone, alone in the midst of so many others, and this diary is my one consolation. It has shared my secrets, and now it shares my sorrows. No word has come from Cyrus, or my village. Other girls get messages from a network of servants bribed by their parents to deliver word from home. Mordecai has so little money; surely he will not waste it on sending word to me about our flocks, or my roses. About Cyrus, he knew so little. How could he know how desperately I long to hear of Cyrus. Has he married as his father wished? Will he come?

The days here pass slowly—not like the days in the market. The girls at home rise early and race the sun to the marketplace. Here, the girls sleep until they are awakened, and would hardly take notice of the sun, except that the servants keep the bath schedule by it. I, however, am wakened early by Niloufar, who brings a tray of tea and fruits, and another servant behind her who carries steaming towels. The servants prop me up gently on my bed, and between my sips of tea and bites of the fruit, they lay steaming towels across my face, bosom and hands. This is not a bad way to wake up, I confess, but the evening ritual has been as unpleasant as the mornings have been gentle.

Every evening, servants corner me and lead me to my bed, where I am slathered in oils and creams. Truly, I am embalmed nightly! There are many oils the servants use, but myrrh is their favored one. (One evening, I complained of a headache, and the girls produced a jar with a baby cobra floating dead along with rose petals and oil. This was applied to my temples. I have not complained since.) Myrrh is used on my face, often mixed with almond oil because the fat stays in the skin for so long. Lotus oil is used on my bosom, and myrrh again on my hands and the rest of my body. Then I am wrapped in strips of clean linen and laid down on my back, hands at my sides, for the night. A servant stands watch over me to make sure I remain in this position, for I must not move my hands in my sleep and disturb the oils of my face, nor must I be allowed to roll over and crease my body.

That is why every morning I am cleansed softly with steaming towels to remove the oils I was embalmed with the previous night, and to steep my skin once more in their mystic powers. And I understand now why I have heard the girls here say the servants from the East are preferred, as any servant from Egypt would scrub us raw in their zeal for cleanliness. These bits of gossip most often come to me by accident, a carelessly loud word spoken beneath my balcony, or echoed from the baths below. Ashtari and Hagai are still keeping me separate from the others, though I long to speak to a girl from my own province. A few others are kept separate as well; I can see them across my balcony. But I have been told my quarters are the most coveted. Hagai is known for choosing wisely, and first.

Only Yoon-Mai is content to see this loft and not abide in it. She loves to stroll the floor and scare the other girls, taking stock of her rivals. There are many servants in the pay of her people from home; she has good accommodations, I am told, and readies herself daily to take the throne. Xerxes will keep all his harems, even when he marries, they say, but I suspect Yoon-Mai will unleash a disaster upon us all if she is made queen. There are two ways to easily kill us in a moment, and these make us all tremble at night: a sudden fire, since we are prisoners with no escape, and a sickness. The girls inspected upon arrival are not only surveyed for their beauty, but for sores and lesions, for a plague could move through us all quickly and destroy us. I have no faith in the healers and magicians that sometimes move among us, feeling our bellies to know when we will be fertile, or smelling our breath to know what humor we may be in. They believe themselves to be diviners of the female spirit, but in truth, they are foolish little men with meaningless spells and potions. Like so much of what I see here, their art is only pageantry, shadowplay with no source or substance.

19

Fifth Day of the Month of Shevat
Seventh Year of the Reign of Xerxes
Year 3398 after Creation

This day was not as taxing to me; am I surrendering or adjusting? I have been stripped by now of all reminders of home—even much of my hair! My clothes are gone, and new ones line the room. Even the smells of home are lost to me now. If Cyrus cannot come, I must plan to escape, but as yet, I see no way, time, or place, for I am rarely alone, and even if I were to venture downstairs toward the main doors, I am too afraid of Yoon-Mai and her tiger to try. Ashtari brought me a mirror to show me the change in my skin since I have been under her care. I marveled at the image I saw; I could not put the mirror down. Ashtari was pleased with my reaction, at first, until my question.

"What did I look like before?" I asked.

Ashtari took the mirror away and stared at me, her brow knotted.

"Was I so different?" I asked, in ignorance. I tried to explain that we had not had mirrors of this sort in my village, and there had been no call for them for a girl who worked in the marketplace. But it was no consolation for Ashtari, who realized her efforts were lost on me for the moment. She busied herself with other matters for the remainder of the day, and I did not see her.

Hagai came to me today with a bowl of figs. Perhaps they were a peace offering. The girls knew how unhappy I was at being here and how poor a student of their arts I am. For I care nothing of scrubbing and oiling my skin, of dreaming of the king's touch or making myself into the soft earth that will bear his seed. Even Ashtari has lost patience with me. I have told no one that I am one of the Jews, or of my love for Cyrus, but these secrets make me as brittle and unbendable to their work as can be imagined. I can only guess what Niloufar is whispering to the other girls, even as she turns her blank smile upon me. But Hagai seemed not to mind.

He set the figs down next to me, and we talked. We talked of little things, which are the best things to discuss when everything else is big. He admired how soft my elbows and palms have become in just a few short weeks. He is so kind. It makes me believe this place cannot be so full of bad omens.

I could tell by the softening of the light through the ceiling that the hour was growing late. Hagai did not rush me into words, and I was able to tell him as much as I could while keeping my secrets. But when I began telling him of my great distress at being offered to the king's bed, that I believed it was wrong to give the body so, that I believed in love and holy marriage above greed and lust, he laid his hand on mine and moved closer. No man but Cyrus had done that in such a manner. I reflexively pulled away.

Hagai frowned and sat back. "Why did you pull away? For what reason do you disdain being touched? Do you not understand you are to give so much more to the king?"

I tried not to choke on the tears hiding just behind my palate. "Hagai," I began, "it is true that I believe much here is wrong. I was not meant for this harem, but it is not just my G-d who tells me so, for in truth, it is my heart that cries out the loudest. Hagai, I could never dream of happiness in the king's bed, because I love another." It was all I could get out. The sobs stayed imprisoned inside, and they burned against my throat and eyes, rioting at being denied their release. I gasped for air, turning away, feeling as if the air were hot ash as it singed my throat and lungs.

Hagai laughed once. "It doesn't surprise me that you love another. Did none of the girls here ever love or live before the king's men carried them away? I know of no one here who dreams of truly returning the king's love. They want his crown, Esther. But tell me, did you think I touched you because I desired you in my own bed?" He snorted a little laugh and his mood began to shift. "Did you think perhaps this was another part of your education, your preparation for the king?" he asked, sounding strange. I could not answer. "Do you not know what I am?" he insisted.

I shook my head. "I did not wish to offend you, Hagai. You prove to be a good and dear friend. But I know nothing of what you are, of this place, these strange customs, and the way girls are thrown to the king every night as easily as wood is tossed into the fire!"

Hagai grew still and formed his words carefully. "You are so naive. You must think the worst burden is to give love when you feel none, but there is another. There are many, many others to fear."

"What burdens do you bear, Hagai?" I asked tenderly. "What have you to fear? Are you not surrounded by luxury beyond imagination, and women so beautiful that the Greeks have yet to match their beauty with their words and epic poems? What harm could ever befall such a powerful man?"

Hagai laughed. I did not understand.

"I am only powerful because I am harmed," he replied. "I was made a eunuch, Esther. Do you know what that is?"

I shook my head no.

"When I was a boy, I excelled at my studies, at my athletics, at everything. I was being groomed for a position of great power, and my parents were eager to acquiesce to the palace. At last it was time for my appointment to the king's service, and so, with many other boys my age, we were led away from our homes. Only we did not go to the palace. We went to an airless, hot home in the countryside, where one by one we were led to a room where a man waited with a table of simple things: a knife, some twine, and a bottle of amber honey. I did not know why the boys screamed, until it was my time. I was laid on the table, a man holding each of my limbs, and stripped. The twine was tightened around my most delicate area, and the knife brought down quickly to sever the organs. Honey sealed the wound. The pain would have killed me, save for the grace of unconsciousness. It did kill many of my friends, however—for every ten brought to this place, only one survived."

I was aware of tears rolling down my face as he talked. He related such awful incidents with a minimum of emotion; how could he be so resigned to such a cruel fate? I had paid a dear price to be brought to this palace, but I could see now that many had fallen to the crown before me.

Hagai sighed as he finished his story and patted me for my own consolation. "The king has indeed entrusted me with all that is valuable to him in his empire. I have earned his trust. You will trust me in time, as well."

I nodded.

Hagai continued "Perhaps you will find a way to make your own peace with the events in your life." He smiled at me softly. "It is true we are all prisoners. But I cannot be sorry you were brought here. I would only be sorry if you wasted your time here. We are all destroyed, everyone, in our lifetime, but few will rebuild. You must redeem your suffering, Esther."

He stood to leave and extended his hand. "The letter that was hidden in your robes the first evening you were brought here? The moonlight will be strong tonight. Perhaps it is the time for you to read it, and then say your good-byes. I have heard of the caravans—that they gave many girls no time for this, so I will be patient with you for one more night. You may keep your diary, for I see it has brought you much consolation. But forget your home, Esther, and Cyrus. Tomorrow, if you are to remain in the best room, under the care of Ashtari, you will awake with a new attitude and a desire to please. I have built on the ashes of my own life by making wise decisions, by knowing what pleases the king. I will not risk myself for a girl who cries in her sleep over a land she will never return to, over boys who were no match for a powerful king and a shrewd father. If you choose this path, tomorrow you will be moved down to the general quarters with the many girls who are not favored to win the crown. They will not view you kindly."

He smiled softly, and bowing before me, left without another word.

Once again my face burned with shame, for I thought no one

would find the scrolls I have kept hidden so well. Hagai has read my scrolls and knows me completely. I trusted Hagai to place me as he saw fit in the harem; now I see I have also entrusted him with my life. It is no wonder he has grown so powerful, when all is laid bare before him, and he can have no part of the riches he guards.

I took the scroll from its hiding place, the scroll Mordecai had slipped to me as I was stolen away from my home. I could not believe that I had left it undisturbed for so long; perhaps it was the hope I could return home again and have no need for a parting letter from Mordecai. I am as foolish as the magicians and healers, thinking if I did not open the scroll, there would be no need for good-byes.

But as I unrolled the scroll, a fresh wave of longing for home swept over me, for this was Mordecai's own hand in great detail, a full page of his own writing! What was it that he had to tell me, but could not, before I was spirited away?

So, my diary, here it is, pressed between these pages, a bit of history that must remain as silent as the graves. How fitting Hagai bade me read it tonight and say good-bye, for I know that when I awake tomorrow, the eyes of the servants will be upon me for my decision. Will I go to the king in splendor or revolt? I cannot bring myself to destroy it, but never again will I read back in the diary, never again will I visit the past in my letters or in my heart. And so tonight I must read Mordecai's letter and seal it in these scrolls as a dead witness to my past:

> *My child,*
>   *As I write this, I know the rumors of the village*
> *carry the weight of truth behind them. You are in*

*grave danger from the throne, and I do not know if
I can protect you. For many nights now I have been
meeting with the elders of our village to discern how
we can protect our girls from the king during the
selection process. I am most concerned for you, Esther,
because of your great beauty. If I had money, you
would have been married off by now, and safe. My
only comfort is that once I protected you from men
who would trade upon your beauty, and so yet I may
do it again.*

*I write this because you must know more of
who you are, of how I rescued you once, and am
prepared to do it again. I had already begun my
return journey to our homeland when your father
died. Your parents, too, had planned on making the
journey, but after your father died, your mother fell
ill as she made preparations for the journey. Oh,
how she loved you, Esther! You were her delight, and
her comfort. Word came to me through a rabbi in
her village that she had been struck by the Great
Fever. I made haste to her village, but she was
already dead. I saw her lying in the street, with
countless others. The sound of the mourners was
unbearable. I raced through the village, calling your
name, asking everyone I saw where you were, but
people were too weighed with grief to keep track of
an orphaned girl. Finally, a sage, who appeared to
be dying as well, told me you had been taken by the*

slave traders the previous day. They had set out west,
toward the palace.

I beat my horse mercilessly; if he had had wings,
he could not have flown there fast enough. I came
upon the traders but stayed in the distance until
I could determine their lot. They made camp and
forced the younger girls to tend to the animals, while
the older girls were dragged inside tents. I could hear
the sound of crying, but did not hear or see you.

I knew these men were a stench in the nostrils of
YWVH. It was not hard to decide to spill their blood.
I wish I could say it was an act of bravery, or great
strength, but in truth, they were greatly preoccupied
with their bounty and did not pay attention to the
muffled screams that came from each tent as I slit
their throats. The girls watched, mute, as I dragged
the men's bodies outside each tent and left them to rot
in the desert sun, to be torn apart by the animals, an
ending as dishonorable as these men themselves. Then
I searched for you, my little lamb! You were asleep
in the blankets, hidden away, and whole. I carried
you outside and set you on my horse. You woke up
slowly, and recognized me as your cousin, for I had
visited your parents before the Great Fever. They had
bought my lambs to add to their own flock as I left
for Jerusalem.

But there was yet a greater problem. These girls,
some of them from my own village where I had lived

*during the exile, would surely know me, know my
name. The throne would send men to kill me for
my act of betrayal, stealing what was not mine in
the king's eyes. So I sent the girls toward the Persian
Sea, where merchant ships come in, hoping that
perhaps they could live unmolested, or find a way
to another country where perhaps women are not so
abused. I found the oldest of the girls, and together
we counted the coins in the pockets of the dead men. I
drew her a map as best as I could and blessed her for
their journey. They had no homes to return to, being
orphans of the Great Fever as well, and traveling
unescorted back to their homelands might mean a
fate worse than slavery.*

    *I took you, and we rode together on a swift horse
until safety was certain. I changed your name from
Hadassah to Esther, and we wandered at last to the
capital of the empire, Susa. It was a city of business,
not bloodshed. No one would suspect what we were
fleeing from. The best place to hide is always in the
open, is it not? The horse, a beautiful stallion (I shall
never forget him), was easily bartered for a flock of
lambs, this being the one trade I knew well, and we
began our lives.*

    *I tell you all this, dear one, that you may know
and never forget the power of the throne, and its
terror, nor the lust of men for flesh and gold. You have
escaped disaster once, you may yet do it again. My*

days spent at the palace gates have bought us more than information; I am learning who is to be trusted in times of peril.

You slept so soundly that night so long ago, surrounded by danger. If all my efforts fail, and you are taken to the palace, you must again learn to sleep among thieves, and when sleeping, find the thread of good woven into your bad dreams. Find it, seize it, follow it. I will do all I can from the outside to secure a good name for us both in the courts, and to procure your release.

I will send word to you again as I find a way.

Your cousin and guardian,
Mordecai[1]

---

1 See the appendix, page 279 for commentary.

20

Sixth Day of the Month of Shevat
Seventh Year of the Reign of Xerxes
Year 3398 after Creation

A storm moved over the harem last night; lightning illuminated our rooms in quick blue flashes, and the sounds roared across the mosaic floors, slapping into the great hinged doors and making the gilded paintings rattle.

I tried to sleep. I knew many would look to see my countenance upon waking; would I remain under Hagai's care, or be lost among the others? I lay in bed weeping, wondering how many below were awake, dreaming of taking this very spot. One night to decide my life: that was what I was given. I could leave Cyrus in the pages of this diary and embrace a wasted destiny, or cling to my dreams and perhaps die alone, waiting for a night with a king or a rescue from a young love, both of which may never come. It reminded me somehow of the boys in the market when tales turned to war, how they would endlessly describe the tortures our enemies visited upon fallen troops. The boys would debate whether it was better to be split open and die from shock rather than pain, or have your heart pierced through and die at once from both. Tonight it was my debate, too.

As I turned over and over in my bed, the storm made the room cool, so I had to slip lower in my bed coverings. The rain began a steady drumming against the roof, and an unseen servant moved a covering coated with pitch over the openings above, so that few drops escaped to reach my chamber. It made all darkness around me, and soon I felt my swollen eyes easing together, my sobs settling into deep breaths, and darkness releasing the hold of this place.

I do not know how long I lay there, sleeping without dreams. A sound caught my ears, but my mind moved so slowly to wake that I listened without moving. Something drew near in my chamber in the night, a strange rustling like a great bird folding in its wings as it alights on the ground. I still could not open my eyes, so deep was my sleep, and a peace flooded my heart. All was well here; my very bones were warmed in some unseen light. A voice, heard as if from a great distance, reached me now, even as I felt the great one departing:

He has not despised or disdained the suffering of the
afflicted one;
   He has not hidden His face from her, but has
listened to her cry for help.
   You will proclaim His righteousness to a people yet
unborn,
    for He has done it.

I knew at once these words; they were from King David, a psalm the Lord had put upon his heart generations ago. I had heard them from our teachers in the village, and now they were meant for me. How I longed to open my eyes and see this visitor of G-d, but the peace was too intoxicating and lowered me again into the sweet silence of heavy sleep.

And so I was awake before my servants even entered the chamber this morning. I was rested, perhaps for the first time. The one who had stood guard over me in the night had fallen into a deep sleep, too, and wiped her wet mouth in an embarrassed rush as she realized I was already awake. I smiled at her. How blessed I am, that when I was too weak to choose my path, an unbidden blessing made my way clear to me.

I stood, and faced the women who entered.

21

Twenty-seventh Day of the Month of Adar
Seventh Year of the Reign of Xerxes
Year 3398 after Creation

My hiding place is ever well hidden now: I will not even write its place. There will I keep only my diary and the necklace given to me by Shethana on my last birthday before I was brought here. I have asked Hagai to send a box with a key to set them inside, and one was delivered by another eunuch with no questions. (How odd it is to know now the truth about the men in this place! I find myself staring too long at each, wondering at the pain and humiliation each survived. It makes me feel faint to think I am soon going to the king who wielded such terrible, thoughtless power. It was nothing to him to lose so many boys. How much less of worth a woman is here, and so how much greater the danger is. The stupid girls so eager to arrive in this place gave no thought to that.)

After the eunuch left I watched carefully to make sure my act was unwitnessed, and I set the diary inside.

Some believe that the spiritual world around us tests us continually to know what we hide in our hearts. They believe the spirits are greedy for human sport, and grow despondent if we cease to entertain. Perhaps it is so: After my good-byes, and the sealing of the second scroll, Mordecai sent a message through the harem guards. It was brief and lifeless, only a little test of his own. He inquired only as to my health and treatment by the overseers. I was not destroyed by this reminder of home; enough strength remained in me from my visitor in the storm that I was able to reply with a firm if quiet voice, and let the servant go again. It was good to know Mordecai was thinking of me, and good to reassure him all was well. But that is all it can be.

Perhaps Hagai knows of this message from home; how could he not? I am Hagai's charge now, not Mordecai's, and Hagai is the master I must strive to please. Of course, if he feels any message from Mordecai impairs his work, he will speak, and I will obey.

G-d forgive me for saying this, even if it only spills onto these innocent and mute pages, but it has been easier to entrust Mordecai to G-d than Cyrus. Sometimes I wonder that the midnight visitor did an incomplete job, to have given me strength but not so much that I stop asking for more. I believe there is a purpose in my being here, I believe G-d has seen and heard, yet I cannot let Cyrus go. I turn him away in my thoughts, and he steals into my dreams. I shove away all memory of him, his touch and his smell, but find he is woven into the fabric of my being. Once I even longed for a moment that Yoon-Mai might indeed find me alone, for in death would I not know freedom from this war? How brave the men once seemed as they marched to war when I was a girl, such valiant warriors carrying their banners and armor in front of them. Yet I know now it is the women left behind who fight the fiercest wars, this daily battle to bury the heart's cries and still live on.

I did not dream that destiny would find me, a girl with nothing of merit to her name (not even her name being truly hers), yet here I am, bidden by the throne of G-d to serve the throne of man. Destiny has an allure only to those she has not called; those who have tasted her find her bitter.

22

Eleventh Day of the Month of Adar II[1]
Seventh Year of the Reign of Xerxes
Year 3398 after Creation

It has been two weeks since I read Mordecai's letter and sealed it away. I have kept my oath never to revisit it. And yet in my mind I have pondered Mordecai's words, turning each over in my mind until I am sure I have wrought every possible truth and meaning from them, like the way I once learned to force the water out of our clothes when washing. So, it seems, I am no stranger to this king, and his drama, although he has never known my name. I believe I am fated to play out this role to its conclusion.

Hagai's words, that I must redeem my own suffering, have rung for days in my head, and as much as I once wanted to continue to mourn and grieve and dream of what could never be, I have begun to feed that strength imparted to me. Mordecai is my cousin and second father; his love will remain constant, I know. I do not need to say good-bye to him as much as I need to breathe in and feel our

---

1 Adar II would indicate that this was a leap year, which generally occurred every three years in the ancient Babylonian calendar.

distance, and make of it what I can. But, oh, when Cyrus comes to me in my dreams, G-d help me, even there now I turn him away. Hagai was right: I am destroyed, and a new creation must arise in her place.

I listen now to what my servant girls tell me, and I rub the almond oil into my skin as faithfully as the most desperate of the harem girls. These girls will give anything to become Xerxes' next queen. I am not fashioned so. Yes, I will learn all here, I will become the summit of all the servants' skill and wisdom, but I will serve as if serving the Lord, not a man. I do not understand the turns in my path, but I am committed to the course now.

But when my mind leaps forward to the night with Xerxes, all goes dark before me. No words of instruction are given to me from heaven. I have only my faith, and the laws of my people, to guide me. I am constrained by the knowledge of a living G-d; I must not allow shame and dishonor to touch me. If I die for this, I die. In this harem, in all the world, it is the same: The men rule and reign, and bid the women dance. To lose step, to fall out of favor and time, whether by age or by design, is to die.

G-d will not be swayed, His laws remain constant. He will give me no quarter to amend myself to this world, and so He may very well see me torn from it.

Yet G-d's light radiates from within me in this dark place. I have been denied my feasts and sacrifices as a Jew, but I feel Him here, like the sense someone has turned the corner just ahead when you enter a hallway. The king has asked for a whore; I will show him a queen. I will not give my body to a man who is not my husband. Moses would stone a woman who behaved thus; even at a king's command it cannot please G-d. If Vashti was banished for the small-est of offenses, I have no doubt I will lose my head for such a bold play if my audience proves too fickle. Yet to lose my life is to join my father and mother again, and so I cannot weep.

The only indulgence of my past I will allow myself now is my prayer. Twice daily I go onto the roof, near my bath, and pray toward my homeland, Jerusalem. I pray for my people who have begun to return there, for their dream of rebuilding the Temple of the Lord. I pray for Mordecai, who has learned well to send secret messages to me through the guards who keep watch over the harem. Mordecai never tells me of Cyrus, and I pray daily for the strength to let him die to me as well. I pray for this strength as often as breathing, but my thoughts still steal away to him on occasion.

Sometimes when I am on the roof praying, I spy other girls in the courtyard worshipping Ahura Mazda, tossing coins to the Magi[2] who come to bless the girls who are soon to go in to Xerxes. His palace is visible just beyond our harem, and it is a beautiful sight, even to me, to see the torches burning every night, and the elite palace guard called the Immortals, leading an elaborately adorned girl out of the harem into the imposing palace. Tigers and lions strain against their chains as she glides past; the clouds circle round the hanging moon as if even that were in the guard of Xerxes. Some girls are so young, they teeter under the weight of gold and the headdress. I keep watch over them as they wind their way to him, and I pray for them as their mothers might have. The girls in the courtyard left behind are

---

2 The Magi were an elite group of men. Some were priests, some were scientists, and some were simply very wise and respected sages. The Magi frequently read the stars for divine messages, and thus it was Magi, or "wise men" who saw the star of Bethlehem that led them to Jesus after his birth.

searching for a savior, and Xerxes is all they know. It weakens their spirits, I can see. I wish I could tell them of YHVH, but Xerxes will not allow any other religion except for his own, the worship of Ahura Mazda. He seems halfhearted in his reproach; it seems more of a political nature to keep peace within his borders. His father, the great King Darius, once issued a proclamation that all people must honor the god of the Jews as the one true G-d. But the time for lenience to us and our ways is over. An evil hand has stirred the sands here.

Last night in the courtyards I spied the opium dealers giving a sinister dark powder to a girl who kept her shawl carried high about her head, wrapped so that none could see her face plainly. She received it gratefully, kissing him on the cheek before returning to her chambers. She seemed so small from my perch; surely her troubles could not have been that large. After all, it is true, and I will say it now, for many of these girls, this harem is a refuge. No harsh weather and toil without shelter, no starvation, never again to see younger siblings sold to cruel masters to feed the others.

But to seek the opium dealers is a dire sign that all is not well for her here. No doubt she was one of the many who have been here too long, too long to dream of Xerxes anymore, and have forgotten how to dream of anything else. Some girls have offended the eunuchs, or the older women who also rule the harem, so they find that their night to see Xerxes will never come. They have spent a lifetime preparing for a feast they can never eat. Opium becomes their dirty angel. They are never allowed to smoke it, for that would ruin their teeth; maintaining the illusion they will one day see Xerxes keeps them alive. Instead they sprinkle it on their food or in their wine.

Beneath me, while I slept, this same girl took the powder, all of it at once. Others found her lying in her bed, vomiting and weak. They slipped her more opium and let her go to her ancestors in peace at last. It was a measured kindness, for of course every servant wants to advance her own girl in this game for the crown. Ashtari related all this to me as simply as another servant might tell me what we would have for breakfast. It was not new to her, opium and death, but the sadness of it stayed with me for hours. There are rumors that some bring about a rival's death in this way if she has excelled in her study of seduction and promises to find favor with Xerxes. I wonder if anyone has ever counted the number of girls who come into the harem, and the number who leave. But nothing of women is ever recorded in this kingdom, unless we give birth to boys. Gold is counted, silver counted, battles counted, men counted, but women are forgotten as quickly as an afternoon breeze.

The calendar year is ending. But what do such dates mean to me now? Almost four months have passed since I was brought here. My time is nearing the halfway mark until my night with the king. I returned from the balcony and, searching in my chamber, found the mirror Ashtari had once used to show me my reflection. The moonlight was high and strong tonight, the clouds being few and distant. I saw myself in the mirror and reached for my reflection. It was so cold. I touched my face, feeling the softness of the work of the myrrh, and the faithful ministrations of the servants. My hair, dark and loose, fell about my shoulders and cascaded down my back. I turned in the mirror a bit to see it. It had been richly scented, and I swung it about to catch the scent of blossoms and fruit. On my first night here, Hagai had said I was a flower that would blossom under his care. He was right, but I did not know what was at the center, I did not know what would unfold before his eyes. I have been forced to live out a dream that was not my own, and it is here I am discovering who I truly am.

I may rot here, or flourish, but remain here forever I will. I am sorry, Mordecai, that you have spent your energy on a hopeless endeavor, not knowing what my fate was to be. I am not here by your hand, and your hand cannot save me. But I hear G-d's voice calling me further on. So under their care, I will bloom as a rose, and any who sway me from His path will find a sharp thorn.

23

First Day of Nisan
Eighth Year of the Reign of Xerxes
Year 3399 after Creation

I saw the girl carried out that day, wrapped in a simple blanket. She was removed as soon as she was proved dead, and I am told she was buried within the first hours, as is the custom here. As I drank my tea this morning, daring to watch from my balcony as the women moved below inside the harem, I saw a girl wearing a certain shawl. I called to her, and she stopped, hearing her name from above.

"Come up to me," I called. She obeyed quickly, which tells me she is of little consequence here, and may never see the king.

"Where did you get this shawl?" I asked, for it was so familiar.

"From the dead one, Yoshtya. The servants said I could take it," she added. I was open-mouthed, struck by the name. She pleaded with me not to turn her in for stealing, and I sent her away with a promise to keep her secret.

I have recorded your name twice here in this book, young one. I have marked your passage, though no one else has. May you find peace at last.

We were from the same province, and not so far from the same age. All that separated us, truly, was our beauty. Mine found immediate favor; hers was slow to reveal itself. It was too slow. Until this place, I had never given thought to my form. My arms were strong and lifted the baskets for market above my head easily. My legs carried me about wherever I cared to go, miles a day. Here, they are praised for their form and nothing else. Yes, it is the most useless parts that get the most lavish praise, my buttocks and breasts, which until now have done nothing for me, and now are the talk of so many. I am created to please a king and no less, this is what they say, and I, too, have begun to see it. I can see that my lips are full, where others' are thin, and my eyes are the shape of new almonds, surrounded by thick lashes. I have heard the whispers since I came to this place; now I begin to believe them.

24

Third Day of the Month of Nisan
Eighth Year of the Reign of Xerxes
Year 3399 after Creation

There is other news, unsettling, which I must relate. I am unsure if I will live to see my night with Xerxes. That is out of my control, and so I am determined to turn those thoughts away when they intrude. It is an art I learn to master again each day. I have set Hagai as a special watch outside my chambers, and no male servant but Hagai can attend me. He also carefully watches over the affairs of my girls, and has already removed Niloufar from attending to me. Fewer people must have access to me, as greater numbers now turn against me. (I will tell you what has happened in a moment.) But Hagai has less time for me suddenly, as the girls who have completed their year here go to the king every night. It took months, Hagai has explained, to bring virgins from every province in Xerxes' empire, from Egypt to India and every stop in-between. Many girls were nearly complete with their year of beauty treatments before I even arrived. Hagai spends the last few moments with each one before they leave his charge forever. He helps them select their robes, and procures for them whatever gift they choose to present to the king. Because Hagai is often away from me, he worries more. Only tonight am I beginning to understand the hidden dangers he sees.

Why, Lord, when I have agreed to play Your game here, why do You taunt me like this?

This is what happened: As I bathed on the rooftop, I spotted the white tiger bounding through the gardens, running for an open gate. He seemed a vision, there in the moonlight, making his run for freedom. For a moment I longed to be a rider on his back, running away from here until his white fur blended into the moon at the horizon. But the screams from down below brought me to my senses quickly, and Hagai burst onto the roof with a dagger, pulling me from the bath to his side. His eyes were wild, and when we heard footsteps coming up the stairs, he motioned for my silence. It was Ashtari, and if she hadn't spoken quickly to ascertain her identity to us as she approached, I am afraid of what Hagai might have done. After her, my other girls filed up slowly, shaken. It seems Yoon-Mai was murdered at her dressing table. Someone set an asp[1] inside her powder box, and as she lifted the lid, it struck. She was to go to the king in two nights. She was so certain of taking the crown; now I am the one favored in this race for a man no one has seen.

I stole a glance below and many cold eyes met mine. One of them was a murderer. "This is not life!" I cried to them. "Life is in the villages, with our mothers and fathers! Life is work, and laughter, and endless toil with sweet little respites!"

No one moved. The servants stopped fanning the girls lounging

---

1 Asp was a common name for any species of small, poisonous snakes found in Persia.

in the waterfall, but only for a moment. A few sideways glances were cast, and the girls were in motion again, gliding toward their baths, or lessons, or meals. Their hatred, or disregard, for me rose from the floor like a wave of heat, and I fell back in tears onto my lounging couch.

All this, and for a beauty I did not ask, did not care for. It is a meaningless thing to me, and yet I see it coveted so. It is not a thing to be shared, else I would have given it away. It is mine, indeed it is who I am, the gift of G-d for my times, a thing given without consent. The long hours of baths and oils have taught me to fix my hope on what does not evaporate into the mist around me. And I find this to be my faith, which, although as ethereal and delicate as a spider's string, can hold forth against bitter winds and violent rebuke.

Even so, I will not sleep easily tonight, although both Ashtari and Hagai will sit vigil over me. G-d help the girl who would kill for a godless king.

25

Fourth Day of the Month of Nisan
Eighth Year of the Reign of Xerxes
Year 3399 after Creation

Ashtari brought me to the edge of my chambers tonight and insisted I peer over the edge.

"Another girl has fallen ill, though she will not die," Ashtari said.

"What am I to see, then?" I asked.

"I suspect you will see your enemy revealed," she answered. "She has moved ahead in the order of virgins presented to Xerxes, since no more stand in her way, and your time is not yet complete."

An Egyptian girl covered in gold coins was being led to Xerxes. Her hair and makeup were splendid, her eyes seeming to extend far back so that she appeared to see all, even as all saw her. Gold snakes coiled around her arms, and her bare thighs were dark, etched with pagan tattoos of henna, leading the eye to the most sacred place of womanhood. She was beautiful, and brazen, and for a moment I doubted my own beauty. (Why is it beauty inspires men, and leaves women troubled?)

In truth, the servants have done such excellent work preparing my body to receive the king's touch; every inch is soft and supple, and my hair is as fragrant and cool as the finest linens on his bed. But only now have I begun the work of making a willing heart to give myself to a king, and no servant can groom my heart. How is it that this girl walking beneath me has mastered herself, willed herself to go proudly to his bed simply because it was commanded on his whim? In the villages she would die for such dishonor. Is it the crown that makes ignoble things good? No, such dishonor is evil, and even great power and wealth cannot mask its scent. I cannot explain it, but I know somehow that is not my path. She is willing, for the king, but defiant to G-d and His law. Perhaps that is where we part ways.

But this girl stopped under my balcony and stared at me with a slight smile. She blew a little kiss and continued on to the palace. As she turned the corner to leave these chambers forever, one of her servants broke free and ran upstairs with a small white box. She presented it to Hagai, then fled back down and rejoined her procession as it left. Hagai opened it carefully, holding it away from him, and I saw him grow hot with anger. I stood and approached him, but he would not show me. Only when I insisted, in that tone Hagai has grown to know, did he show me the box. It was Yoon-Mai's powder box. Inside was the head of the asp.

Perhaps the danger is gone, but it will be another night of little sleep. I wonder how Xerxes will fare with her in his bed. And, suddenly, it brought me great pleasure to think on this: that the king had better please the virgin, or she may save us all the trouble of finishing out our time here!

26

*Thirteenth Day of the Month of Tammuz
Eighth Year of the Reign of Xerxes
Year 3399 after Creation*

Another girl is dead. Hagai brought me news of her death when I told him I had seen her body being carried out of the harem at night. In secret. Hagai tells me it was one of the girls who arrived with me in my caravan here, one of the noisier girls who tormented me about my unkempt appearance. It seems she could not wait to go to the king's bed, for she sought solace in the arms of a palace guard. Her eunuchs must have helped her find access to him. Hagai says they will be killed.

"So she was put to death, then?" I asked.

"No," Hagai told me. "She found herself to be with child and sought the care of a local sorcerer to rid the pregnancy. She knew she would be killed for dishonoring the king in such a way. She took the leaves and flowers from a poisonous plant and made a strong brew, some of which she drank, some of which she used to try to cleanse the womb directly. And, of course, you were witness to her success."

I felt a sadness for this girl. She was more prepared than I to be brought here, but she was not prepared for this life.

Now, dear diary, after I have spent seven months in Ashtari's care, I do not know myself from the first image I saw, as I stare at my reflection in the polished mirrors in my chambers. My hair has been darkened with juniper berries, my nails dyed red with henna, and my eyes resemble those of a cat, arching out from side to side. Ashtari has had me on a strict regimen of the finest flours and fruits, with my meat roasted and infused with cumin, to give my complexion a glow and increase my fertility. If I will have one night with the king, it would be best to try to conceive, she says. Giving birth, especially to a son, would move me up to finer quarters in the wives' harem. I have tried not to think too much about that one night, but of course, that one night is what this entire year is about. Everything I eat, everything I wear and do and say is carefully coached so I will not waste that evening. I have begun to ask Ashtari what the king will do with me that night, and afterward, but her reply is always the same:

"Whatever he wishes."

Day upon day, Ashtari and the girls rub almond oil into my skin, and myrrh, and perfume my hair and my body, before applying elaborate cosmetics and dyes. I am but a canvas for their artistry. I am entering a new phase of my education here. My body and face are perhaps fit for a king, but I must learn the art of a royal seduction.

To this end, they brought a woman to me today that I had only heard rumor of. Her name is Sadira, and she is a very fat woman, with severe hair, her makeup packed into the wrinkled crevasses of her skin, the way moss grows between the stones of the palace walls. Her teeth were yellowed from smoking a pipe she carried with her in her robes, and she breathed heavily as if every movement was labored. Sadira is the woman in the palace harem who teaches the ancient arts of seduction, and only those who are favored to win the crown receive private instruction from her. But she eyed me crossly, as if I was all that stood between her and a good nap, and immediately barked at me to disrobe as I would in the king's presence.

My hands felt like blocks of wood as I fumbled with my robes. I knew nothing of what would please a man. I hated having this mound of a woman watching me, my inexperience becoming more evident, my honor feeling more like shame. To my tired mind, having seen so many strange sights here, she seemed to grow larger and larger, until it was just the two of us there in that hot little room, her glaring eyes and my red cheeks.

"Is that how you will win a crown?" she huffed. I fumbled with the gold clasp on my robe, almost tearing it, and she made an awful noise—it was a laugh that was choked somewhere between one of her chins resting against her throat. She stared at me until I felt the first tears beginning to spill down my cheeks. I hated myself in that moment, for crying in front of this wretch, but my tears are as disobedient as any child, and I could not call them back.

Sadira watched me cry for a moment, noting with pleasure each tear that stained my gown. She seemed to count them, until she found their number to be just right.

"We are ready to begin now," she said, and miraculously, she smiled. It was a fearful sight—I almost wished for her grimace again. Her teeth were yellowed and a thick paste rested between each one, like mortar.

"Resistance to learning, that is, your fear," Sadira continued, "is always best spilled through tears. Let us begin, and you will find this rotting old woman holds the keys to the palace, and a new life, for you."

Here she sprang up, as quick as any of the eunuch boys, and stood alongside me. With a flourish of her hands she began working down the clasps of her own robe, and motioning for me to imitate her. She half closed her eyes, losing herself in this slow trance as she moved through her garments, with me following each of her movements, until at last we both stood only in our linen underwear. Then her eyes met mine, and she barked out another series of choking laughs, slapping her thigh and making it wobble like a drunkard on weak legs.

"Again!" she cried, throwing her robes back on. She danced around the room a bit, waving her arms and choking now and again on a laugh. Honestly, soon I couldn't help but laugh myself. I wasn't sure I understood but laughed more and more, without knowing why.

And so, I learned how to disrobe for a king.

When we finished (which I understood when she abruptly collapsed on the floor on her back, heaving great breaths in and out of her bosom), she once again became the crass creature I first met. Standing with great effort, she jabbed her pipe at my face, and said, "Keep your mouth shut, and practice what I have taught you. I will return tomorrow."

And so she left, and my next set of tutors arrived, carefully skirting Sadira as she made her huffing, windy exit. The next set of tutors seemed small and plain after Sadira, but perhaps it is as well, since they had more complicated routines to teach.

Yes, I am learning to dance, and already, new robes and scarves have been set out for the servants to dress me in when I awake tomorrow. The dance is nothing of what I would expect. Because I am from Xerxes' home region, I do not dance as the Egyptians or girls from the East. The Egyptians swing their hips and invite the man near; the Eastern girls tell stories with their hands and start their seduction in his mind. But the girls of Persia dance a sacred dance, using their arms, moving them softly through the air in a snake's pattern. They are careful never to look the audience in the eye and allow themselves to fall into a type of quiet euphoria, exalting their bodies as sacrifices to Ahura Mazda. This is said to be most pleasing to King Xerxes. This is the dance I am learning, but I do not think of a pagan god, made of wood or stone, as I dance. I will dance better than all of them, but for my G-d, not a king or a block of wood.

27

Fifteenth Day of the Month of Tammuz
Eighth Year of the Reign of Xerxes
Year 3399 after Creation

I heard Sadira coming before I saw her. I had been led downstairs, into a private courtyard, where I was to wait for her arrival. She was lying on a mat, carried in by the strongest of the male servants, and I at once feared for her health.

"Sadira, what has happened to you? Have you been hurt?" I cried out.

Sadira glared at me, like I was a camel without a hump, totally useless to her, and popped a grape into her cavernous mouth. She looked round her mat for her bottle of wine and assaulted it with one great gulp. The servants set her down as gently as their strained shoulders would allow and fled from the courtyard.

"I am fine. Your lesson just interrupted my lunch is all, and I did not wish to abandon it quite yet." Her explanation would have been incredible to me had I not already lived in a palace that stretched my imagination every moment. After a few more bites of food, Sadira closed her eyes, took several peaceful breaths, then extended her hand to me. I joined her on her mat. She offered me a grape, which I declined, so she ate it as she began her lesson.

"You have learned now how to catch a man's eye. Now you must learn to capture his mind. Depending on the man, this may be a difficult task."

"Does Xerxes have a great mind?" I asked.

"He brings a different virgin to his bed every night, my girl," Sadira replied flatly. "He is a drunkard and a glutton. Does this sound like a man of great mental clarity?"

I shook my head no.

"And yet we must prepare you for no less than a king, and so we will prepare you well. Already you have failed the test."

"How?" I asked. "I did not know we had begun!"

"You stare helplessly at me like a calf rooting for an udder. Do you really think I would enjoy your dark begging eyes staring at me? You must learn to look away, while keeping me the focus of your attention. Only look me directly in the eye if you truly must."

"Yes, Sadira, I will learn." I said this while looking at her, then caught myself and turned my gaze away quickly.

"You have failed again!" she barked.

"But I looked away as soon as I caught myself!" I replied.

"You are never to speak until you have taken a deep breath and released it. Your words should be slow and soft. Never has a woman here said anything so important that she needed her full voice."

I breathed in and released it, keeping my eyes on Sadira's mat instead of her. "Slow and soft," I repeated.

"Your voice must never carry to the walls; it should be soft enough to hang about you like a gentle fragrance." Sadira's words sounded rehearsed and weary. I wondered how many poor girls had received this same advice and where they were now.

"Yes, Esther," Sadira continued, "every act of love begins as a story, and you are the storyteller. Your eyes, your voice, must invite him into the story. Use whatever the gods have given you to tell the tale. If there is a table, run your fingers slyly along its length. Will he imagine it as your fingers along his spine? Remind yourself constantly of what makes you a woman—brush your fingers along your lips, along your bodice."

Suddenly Sadira barked out another laugh and took a swig of wine from the bottle. She looked me right in the eye. "As if a woman needs to be reminded of what sets her apart. What fool of a king needs a woman who has to double-check to make sure her lips or her bosom are still there? And yet it is you who will play the fool, and perhaps wear a crown. Tell me, Esther, if you do wear the crown, will you rule as a queen, or a jester?"

I could not think of an answer. Sadira loved that.

"Very good! Never answer a difficult question. Just touch your bosom and smile, and he'll forget why he asked." Then Sadira screeched for the male servants to come and carry her away. As they approached her mat, she tossed me a little cluster of grapes.

"Good luck, young one." She smiled.

A small horror struck me. If this was to be my last instruction before my night with the king, it seemed many details had been omitted.

"Sadira!" I protested as she was being lifted into the air. "Sadira, no one has taught me how the story ... ends. No one has taught me what to do when he reaches for me!" It was as modest as I could express myself, although now I wonder if my modesty is lost on my companions here.

Sadira spoke over her shoulder to me as she exited, tossing her words as casually as she tossed the grapes. "My dear, some things the king would prefer to teach you himself."

28

Third Day of the Month of Kislev
Eighth Year of the Reign of Xerxes
Year 3399 after Creation

My year is nearly done. If I am lax in writing down the events of my days here, you must forgive me, my diary. The last three months have been an endless repetition of baths, perfumes, cosmetics, and oils. All has been quiet and no more deaths have occurred. (I am assuming that the murderous rival has not become queen, else Xerxes would not continue his quest for the perfect virgin. Yet I have been here long enough to know he may never find her, and may well enjoy us all in his time.)

And this is my second plea to you to forgive my lack of writing: that there are some things not fit to print, that would curse the pen and paper just to receive the words. When I see the other girls in the harem walking around naked, proud, and senseless, I can only avert my eyes in shame, a shame they will never feel. The eunuchs tell wild stories of debauchery, and indeed there are eunuchs who do more in service to the royal courts than I would have cared to know. Niloufar has had her right hand chopped off this week for being found with a eunuch in an unspeakable act. There is no limit to imagination here, I must say.

Why would G-d bring me to this place? Surely Mordecai was right when he called this people godless, for G-d is far removed from them. But if I walk among them, does G-d still see me? I cannot imagine that He would turn his eyes toward this palace of sex and intrigue. But I will serve him, even here, even if He cannot bear to hear my prayers. When I pray, I go out onto the roof, where Ashtari has learned to give me my peace and I can be alone with G-d, as far above the godlessness as I can go. Only Mordecai's letters strengthen me to remain true to my heart for G-d, even as it seems I have been forgotten.

Oh, Lord, they are teaching me things here I should never have known. My night with the king is fast approaching, Lord, and forgive me if I almost welcome it! I know I will ask for the crown, and if it is not given, I will be forced to lie with him anyway. I see it is only one final night of degradation. I fear my desire to act in honor is weakened at moments by the lure of being free of this place, of doing what is expedient in my cause. Yes, I will act in honor; yes, I will ask for the crown before the bed, but I confess I care not sometimes whether I give or am taken.

In this place, I've grown to love Ashtari and Hagai. It's true; never have such kind and good souls lived among such refuse. But I want to be free of this house of prostitution ... for that is what it must seem to you. When I move on to the wives' harem, I must hope it will be different. These women do not have the burden of winning a crown; indeed, they will never see the king again unless called to him by name. Hagai says that Shaashgaz, the eunuch in charge of the wives, is a much happier man than Hagai himself is. The wives do not bicker so much, nor do they preen so proudly and order the eunuchs about in service to their whims. They are more settled and secure, and Shaashgaz says that friendships flourish there as the blessed ones tend to their children. So, Lord, if this is what you have planned for me, I will go there. Just remove me from this den of intrigue. Send me where there won't be a thousand whispering voices, and clandestine meetings by candlelight, and enemies hiding in the shadows. And if it please You, allow me to conceive on this one night of shame, so that I may live my days in honor at last.[1]

---

1 See the corresponding commentary on page 280 of the appendix.

29

Second Day of the Month of Tevet
Eighth Year of the Reign of Xerxes
Year 3399 after Creation

"What is he like, Hagai?" I asked.

Hagai frowned as he turned to answer. "He is a man, Esther, no more. But he is a man with the means to satisfy every desire, and so he has become dangerous."

I urged Hagai to continue.

"A lion in the wild hunts its meat, and the men in the village understand the beast. There is harmony. But your Xerxes is like a caged lion; his supper is thrown to him. He has become bored, fat, and unpredictable. You must be the lioness that awakens him again."

"How will I do that, Hagai?" I asked.

"She is smaller, but more stealthy. She controls the hunt with her eyes, always watching, weighing, waiting. She will always know the moment to strike. But there must never be a confrontation of power, for the male lion is unable to distinguish between enemies."

"I still don't understand what that means to me, Hagai." I sighed.

He kissed me on the cheek. "You will."

And yet I had one last question: "What shall I take into the king, Hagai?"

He paused, and I knew the treasures of the kingdom passed before his eyes. He looked at me and smiled. "You are enough for any king."

I forced a smile back. I must believe that.

30

*Twenty-ninth Day of the Month of Tevet
Eighth Year of the Reign of Xerxes
Year 3399 after Creation*

As I was led down the corridor to the king's chambers, I could feel the eyes of every man in the palace on me. The oldest guard placed his hand upon his chest and bowed his head, a gesture that said my beauty had won a heart. I saw a few gold coins being wagered, passed down the row to another guard for safekeeping. It told me Hagai's words were true: I was just another piece of meat being thrown to a caged lion. Their roving glances at me would not have been so free if they earnestly believed this was a game that could be won, that I might become queen.

My scarves blossomed out as I walked along, the rich red silks setting off the copper and gold jewelry, making me look like the morning star before a red sunrise. I caught scent of my perfume as the breeze moved among the columns of the corridor. I had been anointed in the most unlikely places with a perfume made from lotus flowers, set in the oil from a crocodile. The lotus flower was an aphrodisiac, and Ashtari told me the oil would impart to me the unmatched power of the crocodile. All has been done to assure that I might conceive tonight. I have been stuffed and rubbed and washed with herbs of all varieties, and when the Magi came in to anoint me with spells and magic for my womb, only then did I refuse their entreaties to prepare me.

Ashtari gave me a bracing, strong wine to drink before she bade me farewell. I did not know why I should need to dull my senses before such an important night. Ashtari's tone in reply was measured; I could tell she did not want to unravel my tightly wound nerves. "You are going to a man's bed for the first time, Esther," she replied. "You must expect there will be pain. Only I would caution you to smile throughout, or at least avert your face if you cannot. You would not want the king to think he did not enrapture you." A smile was playing on her lips and I tried to smile back. I smelled the brew, as not to offend her, but it stung my eyes and I thrust the cup back to her at once, without tasting it.

Saying good-bye to Ashtari was much more difficult than I had imagined. On this night of good-byes, my heart is aching. I cannot seem to stop myself from thinking, too, of my love, Cyrus. It is his bed I should be going to. My body should have been prepared for him, for our wedding night, not as another offering to a gluttonous king. Cyrus had awakened me to love; it is cruel that this other man should be my lover. But G-d help me now, for this battle in my mind is overwhelming, and I must be free to do what I came for. At least I have this small comfort: Just as Mordecai was able to spirit messages to me inside the harem, he will find me wherever I may go after tonight. I will not lose that.

Hagai led me farther down the great hall, until we stood

underneath a great frieze of running horses. It was three times larger than life, and I was struck by the splendor of the king's palace. No wonder this was an idolatrous people, when the king lived in a palace more fitting for a god than a man. My knees began to feel pained and weak.

Hagai paused at the massive set of carved cedar doors just beyond the frieze, and let go of my hand, forever. "Our journey has ended, my child." He smiled. "Do everything I have instructed, and I will pray to the gods for your favor."

I pressed my hand back into his. "There is only one G-d, Hagai. It is YHVH, G-d of the Jews. Promise me that long after I am gone, you will not remember me, but this G-d. Then I will have served you well, my dear friend."

Hagai bent down to kiss me on my cheek. "I will always remember how you loved this God of yours, how He calmed your raging heart. You are a woman any god would proudly claim. How He must be smiling tonight." Then he whispered, "The lion awaits."

I wished now I had accepted the strong wine from Ashtari.

I entered the darkened chamber slowly, as fear fought to control my legs. I kept my eyes low, but I could see attendants milling about, preparing the chamber. There was a large ornate bed, and a basin with water and herbs, and a table of scrolls with golden endpieces that sparkled in the moonlight that crept in, humbly, from a hole in the roof. Was even the moon afraid to disturb this man?

"Come in!" was the king's sharp command.

Servants began to withdraw immediately, save for two Immortals, soldiers with frightening axes who guarded Xerxes night and day, even in the intimate moments of his life. Seeing me enter and approach the bed—this was a drama they had learned well, night after night. I knew I was to enter his bed, silently, crawling under the linens from the foot of the bed, and lie there, awaiting his advances. But I will crawl for no man, and certainly not enter a bed from the foot. I will not disgrace myself to exalt this king. If I die for breaking with the traditions of weaker women, then at least I die having known dignity.

I walked to the center of the room and stopped. I did not raise my eyes, but I could see the outline of a pile of floor cushions behind a sheer veil parted to one side. There, in the center, must be my king.

"What is this Hagai has brought me tonight?"

I paused. "I do not understand your question, my lord."

"Who are you?" was his impatient reply.

"I am called Esther."

"Ah, Esther, like the stars. A woman who is above all." I could not tell if he was mocking me. "Tell, me, Esther, which star were you named after? Can you point it out?" He gestured toward the open balcony.

"No, my lord. My mother died when I was but a child. She did not have time to tell me such things." (My mother would never have known me by this other name. It was she who named me Hadassah.)

"And your father?" he demanded.

"My father is dead, too, my lord. The Great Fever that swept through your empire took him without warning."

"Well, you must be exceptional to have been brought to me so early in the selection process."

In truth, he must have had a thousand women by now from the new harem, besides his unnumbered wives.

He continued. "Let me see your face."

I raised my face slightly into the moonlight, turning it gently in each direction. I was careful not to look at him.

"Undress."

I couldn't help it. I glanced at him suddenly now, before sending my eyes back to the floor.

Xerxes laughed out loud. "A harem girl is shy?"

I chose this moment and looked directly at him. "I am not shy, my lord. I know why I was brought here. But am I goods that must be displayed before haggling in the market? No. I will not trade in my own flesh. You have bought me, and I am yours."

I bowed low to him and retreated to the balcony. My knees were still trembling, and I felt faint. I gulped in the night air and prayed for wisdom. *It is not Xerxes who is the caged animal,* I thought, *it is I!* "Gracious Lord," I whispered to the night sky, "I do not dare dishonor You, but I must please the king as well. Direct his heart, Lord, and direct my steps."

I felt him come up behind me on the balcony. The wind carried his scent to me—oils and cloves—and a musk scent like the sun when it lit on the cedars. I turned to him now and faced him with a soft expression. I let my shoulders drop as I breathed deeply, trying to regain my balance, and my robe began to slide gently off one shoulder. I was too afraid to move it back into place as I watched his expression.

He raised one eyebrow as he followed the line of my body beneath the robe. He reached out and set the robe back into place. I tried to remember to breathe. I did not think he would force himself on me. In the moonlight I was able to look at him clearly. He was much older than my sixteen years, of course, but perhaps only in his thirties. His hair was black, thick, and wild, swept back in a wave from his forehead. His face was quite square; it looked to be chiseled from an unyielding piece of granite, as if the artist had grown tired of the resistance and left the rough edges. His lips were full, but I could see the deep lines already setting in on his face and brow. I wondered if I would have found him attractive when I was a girl in the market.

I found myself wondering, too, that this was the man so many women would have trampled me for. But then, it was not him, but his kingdom that they yearned for. The king and I, we were each a commodity. His eyes were sharp and knowing as he looked at me, like the eyes of the hardest dealers in the market, who refused to sell for lesser prices. I found my thoughts, the year spent imagining this man, tumbling down and taking shape, the way rocks slide in a sheet down the mountain and take another shape when settled. Everything fell into place and shape around this new form, this near and present man who had existed to me only in my mind. I felt comforted to see he was truly a man, and not a god. But my footing was not secure here, either, and my thoughts gave way and tumbled down again, as I saw that he was like no other man I had known.

"Tell me, my Star," he asked, turning out to face the evening sky, "tell me what the women in the harem say about me."

I was grateful my harem year had not dulled my mind as it spun madly for an answer. "I was told you are a lion of a man, and that every girl goes on to the wives' harem a happy woman, having seen your glory." There was enough truth to sound true to him, and enough deception so that I had to suppress a smile.

"And what do you say about me?" he asked, tracing my face

gently now with his finger as he turned and moved closer. I did not like having a man, who was unknown to me, be so familiar, but then, I was only a harem girl.

"It is true that I have never seen such splendor in a king's palace. (Oh, in truth, dear diary, I had never seen any palace before!) But I cannot speak to whether you are a lion or not. I have seen only men, and you are a king."

"Well, let me be a man then, and not a king, and render your verdict in the morning," he replied, with a sly laugh, as he slowly removed his crown and royal robe. He took off his signet ring and set it on the table of scrolls.

I knew he liked my answers; I could sense him toying with the hunt. But something else was stirring in him, a restlessness that made him unhappy. He pointed now to the scrolls, and picked up a large, detailed one. He unrolled it on the bed and motioned for me to look at it.

"Did they condition more than your body in the harem?" he asked.

I did not understand his question.

He spoke again, impatient. "Do you like riddles?"

I nodded slowly.

"Then tell me, Star, what this means. I was defeated in Greece by a simple treachery. We outnumbered them by thousands, yet they forced the battle onto a narrow pass; only a few of my men could fight at once, and so my might was useless. And then a trick so raw, so brute, it has never ceased to needle at me, even as I sleep: They set fire to their largest ships, and used them as ramming weapons against our own fleet. These majestic ships, meant to transport their troops, instead became the means of our destruction, even at the cost of their own lives. Who would have thought to use a ship this way, except the most desperate and weak? Why was I unable to avenge my father's name, and the great name of Persia?"[1] He growled his last words and I could tell he wanted to taste revenge. Rumors in the harem told that he had indeed already exacted some measure of repayment, by burning the fair city of Athens to the ground.

"My lord, if you will permit me to speak on matters I have not been trained in"—and his glance told me he would be so amused— "I must believe this is for the best."

His steel gaze made fear shoot through my legs again.

"My lord, every province as far as the eye, or even the mind can stretch, belongs to you." I gestured toward the balcony and led him there slowly by his hand. "Can you see anything that you do not possess?"

Together we stared silently across the gardens, toward the horizon of the empire.

After a moment I continued. "You are indeed a great lion, who has taken all the prey of these plains. You rule the world, and Greece is now but a mouse to keep you amused. The mouse will keep your claws sharp, and your instincts intact. He is no threat, so I would urge you to enjoy his game."

He was quiet as he took in my reply carefully. "Well done, Star. You are wise. How is it possible that you are a woman? What have

---

1 King Darius had attempted to conquer Greece, but his own fleet was destroyed off the coast of Greece. According to reports by the BBC, a local Greek fisherman raised two bronze warriors' helmets in 1999 along with his catch. Experts believe the fisherman located the spot where the fleet of Persian war vessels sank, and are currently attempting to locate further artifacts.

they taught you in the harem? I understood the subject to be more carnal," he continued as his hand reached for the sash of my robe.

I backed out of his reach quickly, into the room, but with a smile of my own. "My lord, some things cannot be taught. I was brought here tonight to be another of your conquests, wasn't I? But you are not the only one who knows how to go to war."

Xerxes was fully alive now, his eyes glittering and his skin flushed. "You are at war? What, or should I ask who, do you desire to conquer?"

"Perhaps I came to conquer a king, but discovered a man."

I moved away from him, toward the other side of his bed. His eyes never left mine. I held him with my gaze and removed my outer robe. "Women give you their bodies every night in this bed. But who has ever given you her heart? Your crown may give you the right to my body, but you will have to fight for my heart," I said as the lion began to circle me slowly.

"Why should I fight for a woman's heart? I have their bodies. That is enough for me. And why should you want the man? If you give me a child tonight, will you not live a life of unimaginable ease? Why complicate the matter by asking for the man as well?" he replied calmly.

Hagai was right—I knew my moment to strike.

"You are alone in this palace, King Xerxes, as I am," I told him. "Your women want only your money; your advisers want only your crown. Who have you to trust? Who has ever loved the man, and not alone the crown? And who will love this woman, not alone her body?"

"You would not relinquish your heart, even as I take the body?"

Xerxes asked, surprised but in no way alarmed. "So tell me, Star, how will I win your heart? Is it a matter of gold, or do you prefer the flattering words of a suitor? Have I had so many women in my bed only to forget what they want? Tell me your price, and let us come to an agreement at once," he said, moving the scroll from the bed to the table as his eyes followed me with certain hunger. The kingdom, his empire, seemed to lie at my feet now.

"Oh, I am afraid it is a price that is above even you, and the wealth of all your treasuries," I replied.

He seemed to grow impatient now, and I feared I was testing him too much. "Esther," he sighed, "women's flesh is but a hobby for me, an amusement. Why must you treat it as sacred? Lovemaking is only a fleeting pleasure."

My voice grew deep, from somewhere inside. "I am a woman, created in the image of the one true G-d. I will lay His glory at the feet of no man, and for no fleeting pleasure. To touch me is to touch the eternal."

He did not speak. I could not tell if he was angry at the delay, or if my words were finding their mark. He did not even seem to question which G-d I could be referring to in this pagan land. But again he sighed, and rubbing his temples wearily, he asked me again, "So, tell me of your price, my dear. What ransom must I give now for your heart, and thus your body tonight?"

"There is only one ransom for a woman's heart," I continued, "and that is … love, given in honor. That is the price I would ask of you. I am not naive, King Xerxes. You may yet take my body tonight. I have no true choice in that matter. But my heart is mine alone, and I will not leave it behind tomorrow morning. "

Xerxes was silent for a moment. "Every woman who comes to my bed comes only by my money's bidding, and by my money's keep, that is true. But you, Esther, you would come for the man, and not the king? You would be won by only love, and not gold?" he asked.

I did not reply but merely met his gaze evenly.

He looked out across the courtyards into the night sky. "It is true I have no one in this palace, although many are my companions. Three attempts have been made on my life so far, and I have an heir in exile who will surely rise against me one day. I have faced rebellions from Egypt and Babylonia, and the failure of my men to conquer Greece. What can I offer you, Esther? There is no security here, no peace. You say you want only love. But to all others, my queen will only be respected, never loved. She will never know deep, restful sleep, and will never know when her time will be over. I may be away tending the kingdom, sampling my harem, or lying dead in the palace as an assassin comes for you. So again I ask you, Esther, will you come for the man, and not the king?"

When I nodded, he made a decision. The Immortals guarding the chamber, their faces expressionless throughout the evening, now glanced at each other.

He turned, picked his ring off the table of scrolls, and walked steadily to me. I was against the edge of the bed with nowhere to move now. Taking my hand in his, he placed the ring on my finger. He was so close, I could smell the deep earth of his chest. His body became a dark fortress as it encircled me and drew me close, and at last I could let my weak knees give way. His breath was hot as he whispered in my ear, "Then I will not take the body, if I cannot have your heart. Give both to me tonight, and be my queen."

I looked at the ring on my finger, as my legs grew soft from his near presence and manner. I struggled for the breath to ask one last question. Somehow I had always expected to marry in the way of my people, yet I forgot that this king was not even a Jew. My heart was beating too fast, my mind spinning away even as my body gave way to his; the great lion was at last taking his prey.

"Is that all there is, then? Am I now your queen?" I asked.

Xerxes smiled, letting down the strap on my shoulder. "My little Star, tonight you will learn much. Are not my words the law of this land? Yes. You have won your request, and I have won a bride."

We needed no more words that evening.[2]

---

2 See corresponding commentary on page 282 of the appendix.

31

Thirtieth Day of the Month of Tevet
Eighth Year of the Reign of Xerxes
Year 3399 after Creation

A servant woke me up this morning, and for a moment, I believed I was in the harem. Instead, the servant brought in a tray of hot tea and cakes made from raisins, with little slices of flat bread and a thick butter. She set it at the bedside and exited quickly. I sat up in bed, but Xerxes was gone. How strange to wake up without immediate attention to my grooming and care.

I looked down at the ring on my finger. How different it looked, how different everything looked, in the morning sun. All my thoughts this past year had focused on last night. Now I am here, and I do not know what to do.

I am irritated that no one prepared me for these moments after I had been received by Xerxes. And I wished to have seen their faces when they heard I had won the crown. But there is little time for imagining any more. I must call a servant, find fresh robes, and begin my adventure anew.

32

Sixteenth Day of the Month of Shevat
Eighth Year of the Reign of Xerxes
Year 3399 after Creation

I have been brought to the king many nights now. I have had to forget what they taught me in the harem about seduction. I must learn how to love, but my heart is a most unruly child, and I cannot force her to fully love this man yet. For I have decided, resigned myself as Hagai has done, that if I will be called to this man's bed so many nights, I will learn to love him. It is the only way I can redeem myself, my suffering. Strangely, I feel closer to Hagai now. I am a eunuch in my own way; what was precious and vital to me was severed by the crown's command, making me more fit, and more governable than a whole woman might have been. I was destroyed, but I will rebuild, even here, even now. I will love again. A shadow of guilt still hangs about me as I write those words, as if the wind might carry them to Cyrus and wound him. I am stupid to even imagine he still waits, or cares. Men are more resolute in their affections—that is plain to see when I am near Xerxes. They decide to love or abandon, and it is finished.

My nights are the king's, but my days are my own. I have
wandered the queen's palace (my palace!) endlessly. It was once the
beautiful Queen Vashti's—now the native queen is an exile, and an
exiled Jew is in her bed. It all remains a mystery to me, how my
days have fit together into this new life. Of course, I have told no
one that I am a Jew. Only Mordecai, G-d, and this diary are witness
to my deception. King Solomon said once that there is a time for
everything under the sun; Mordecai tells me I must not reveal my
heritage until that time has come. Mordecai still slips messages to me
through the palace eunuchs, and he counsels me in the gossip of the
palace, and how I must continue to conceal that I am a Jew. But I am
not unhappy as I wait. My days have been filled with the preparations for the royal coronation and feast. Xerxes, in celebration of my
crowning, has released everyone in the province of Susa from paying
taxes for this year. I can only imagine what the reaction in the streets
must have been.

I try not to think about those streets. The joy of the coronation
conceals a small matter: My freedom is forever gone. As the Queen
of Persia, I will remain in the queen's palace for the remainder of my
days. If there was ever a hope of seeing my cousin Mordecai again, or
of feasting my eyes on the boy whose memory still runs through my
veins, they are surely gone now. Only at the coronation will the public—the noble and ruling public, that is—have a chance to lay eyes
on me. After that, my beauty and my days will be for the king's lei-
sure only. But I try not to think about that. Mordecai stays close to
the palace at night to bring me word from the village. I am able to send
a servant to fetch his messages and deliver bits of my news to him. For
all that weighs on my mind, however, one great joy has been given

me: I am allowed to choose my servants and staff. I have selected my handmaidens from the harem, including Ashtari. It was wonderful to embrace them all again. As the date for the coronation approaches, the loose threads of my life are slowly entwining into their final, glorious design. G-d has exalted the orphan and defended the cause of the powerless. Were my story to end here today, I would be content to know only that G-d is all, and is in all.

33

Twentieth Day of the Month of Shevat
Eighth Year of the Reign of Xerxes
Year 3399 after Creation

Today is the coronation! We have all been moved to Persepolis, a more fitting place for such a great pageant. Save for an extra nap, and herbs to soothe my swimming stomach, I have passed the hours in much the same way as I did that fateful day well over a year ago when I was first brought here as a harem girl. Already I have been scrubbed and sloughed, petals rubbed vigorously over my body to impart their cloying scent. Ashtari has had me chewing cloves for my breath and my sickened stomach. My mouth is sore! I begged her to let me switch to something else, maybe the resin I have seen the maidens chewing, but instead she gave me lemons. My mouth may be on fire, but she is seeing to it that my breath will be sweet for the king. After my bath, the girls swept my hair up on top of my head, the strands held together with jewels and ropes of rubies. My robe for tonight is pure blue, tied with a white sash around the waist, and a mantle of rubies and gold chains to be worn on top of that.

I am nervously awaiting the call to begin the procession. We will, my maids and I, all be led out and into a caravan made of gold and alabaster. The columns all around it are woven, it seems, out of squares of ivory and ebony. The silks the king has imported from his provinces in the East have been woven into his royal insignia as they drape down, concealing me from the curious crowds.

Just before I step out, Ashtari has promised to weave a fresh red rose into my hair as well. It makes home, and Mordecai, seem near. When I am longing for home, I often send a eunuch to collect the roses from my home. True, the gardens here are filled with flowers, but no rose is as sweet as the ones I once grew. Now they have gone wild and untended, but the eunuch never questions me. After all, these were the roses once sent to the banquet Xerxes threw in his third year.

Wish me your best—this may be the most exciting moment I will ever have, and I will need to cherish it again when our times have grown cold.

34

Twenty-first Day of the Month of Shevat
Eighth Year of the Reign of Xerxes
Year 3399 after Creation

I am lying alone in my bed now, having been left by the king at last. Is it immodest to say I need sleep? Xerxes is a man who rules the world and yet is fascinated by something just out of his reach. My honesty, in all matters except the one, draws him to me. But he is a man without limits. He drinks to excess, he refuses to sit still and listen to reports from the smaller provinces, he still sleeps with the girls from the harem nightly. He is a man given over to his appetites. But I believe he has a noble heart, even if buried under the layers of indulgent ease. I worry what will become of his careless attention to the kingdom.

But I am talking of Xerxes and I mean to tell you, diary, of the coronation itself. Sleep is pulling gently at my eyes, so let me finish this quickly and leave it with you.

I rode in my royal caravan toward the palace at dusk along the great Royal Road. Villagers came out, laying fragrant branches in the road before the carriage, weeping with joy and tossing gifts into the caravan such as spiced nuts and bundles of dried flowers. I could not reveal myself to them, of course, but oh, to be among my people again, even if secluded behind a veil! I tried to breathe in their very essence, and hoped that Mordecai was among them. Perhaps he even ran alongside the caravan, as some of the young boys did. My maids peeked out from time to time to give me reports. They were merry and free, and taken with all the pageantry of the moment.

When we slowed as we entered the palace gardens, we heard the gates close behind us, and a more somber mood overcame us. We had all waited for this moment, and I knew a few had even imagined themselves in this dress many nights as they dreamed. I tried to give every girl a word of encouragement as we readied for the ceremony and encouraged them to later take their fill of the gifts left in the caravan.

When the veil was parted, the palace guards sat at attention on their horses, torches flaming against the late night sky. This was the Gate of All Nations that Xerxes himself had commissioned. The gate sat between two monumental staircases paying homage to Ahura Mazda. Carvings from every nation in the world lined the staircases; I saw such a marvelous collection of peoples there, of all shapes and manners. I was led through the Gate to the Great Hall of One Hundred Columns. The Hall was even more impressive than the Gate, for every panel featured a carving of Xerxes in combat. Was this the gentle man I had met in his chambers? The warrior's eyes followed me from every corner as I was led into the palace by a man named Hathach, followed by my maids with their heads bowed and walking side by side. Guards stood at attention, swords drawn, as we proceeded down an enormous corridor toward a set of double doors large enough to hold the sun itself prisoner inside. The doors were carved with trees and flowers and a river that wound through them all. Then Hathach turned to me and bowed, and swept open the doors.

How can I describe what I saw? Imagine the most splendid hall, filled with flowers of all types of scents and colors. The gold and silver and jewels that adorned every object and every guest shone so brightly I wanted to cover my eyes. Candles dripped their thick wax from sconces all along both walls. There was my king waiting for me, and all eyes turned to me as I began my slow walk toward him. I could feel everyone trying to drink in all the details of my face, what I wore, how I smiled, but most especially, I could feel the king's pleasure when he knew the crowd was awed. Truly, if they did not consider me beautiful, my jewels alone would have outshone them all and should have made them gasp.

I ascended the steps to join Xerxes, his eyes never leaving mine. I bowed and knelt before him. He took off his royal crown and placed it on my head, then returned it to his own. He knelt by my side, and taking my hands in his, kissed them softly. In that most precious of moments, I thought I detected the scent of a harem perfume on his clothes, but I closed my eyes tightly and forced the thought from my mind. I am sure the guests saw a woman caught up in the rapture of the king!

He removed a sword from his side, engraved with the insignia of his throne, and sliced a loaf of bread on the altar into two halves. He fed me my half as I fed him his, and we sipped an intoxicating spiced red wine from a cup that bore both our names. I had been made queen by his word that first night in his chamber; now the people witnessed his law and approved.

When we turned to face the crowd, a roar of approval went up. We descended the stairs and moved through the people once more, toward the palace. Great boxes, covered in beautiful cloth, opened suddenly, startling me. I grasped Xerxes' arm in fright and he laughed. The boxes contained hundreds of birds each, which shot toward the sky in the anger and indignity of being confined in this way. Seeing them scatter and chide us loudly, I laughed now too. A servant handed each of us a heavy necklace of coins, and I watched Xerxes as he unstrung the coins easily and tossed them into the crowds. I followed suit, looking around for the youngest ones present.

The people would go on to the feast being prepared at that very moment, but it was custom that Xerxes and I would not join them until after midnight, when we would then feast and drink until we greeted the first dawn of our official reign together.

His arm encircled my waist, and he led me to the palace. His bedchamber had been prepared for us, and we were alone once more. Roses were everywhere; fresh blossoms, dried petals, and a steaming bath made from rosewater. Persia was indeed the kingdom of roses, their luxury not wasted on Xerxes. But tonight Xerxes had so much more on his mind than lovemaking. I sampled the tray of cheeses and grapes set out, and poured each of us wine into goblets commissioned for this night. He waved away whatever I tried to present to him. I settled onto the covered bench near the bed to wait for his command.

He seemed to burn with an intense desire to reveal something to me, and I waited patiently as his words formed slowly. He walked through the chamber, his hands lightly resting on the precious serving pieces and pitchers. I did not know how much was the same from the coronation of Vashti. Where was his mind now that he was back in these chambers but the queen was new? Finally, he turned to face me.

"I inherited my throne, Esther. My father, Darius, had no legitimate claim to it, did you know that?"

I shook my head that I did not know the story of Darius's rise to power. I wanted to tell him that I knew all about Darius and his kindness to the Jew named Daniel, who survived being tossed into a lion's den, but I feared that would reveal too much.

Xerxes continued. "My father, Darius, was one of a council of nobles. They had grown angry at the vile life of Cyrus the Great's son, who had taken the throne. So the son was murdered, although no one claimed to have knowledge of how it had happened, or by whose hand. But someone had to quickly take the reins of the kingdom if it was to survive. The nobles, after much wine and feasting, rejoicing the death of the son, looked upon their horses, standing in a circle around the campfire. The men decided that whichever horse whinnied first at sunrise, his owner would be the new king. My father was a clever man, and held his drink better than the rest. Even so, I do not know how he did it, but his horse was indeed the first to trumpet the sun's rise."

Xerxes laughed, thinking of the story now. "That horse never worked a day in his life again!" he said between deep, laughing breaths. I laughed too, and wished now Darius had lived a longer life. I would perhaps have cared for him.

"He must have been both clever and strong," I said.

"Ah, but, Esther, it was a hard lot he had bought into." Xerxes grew more somber now and continued his tale. "My father fought

wars and put down insurrections all of his life and finally died as
he had lived. But I have a new dream for a new world. I dream of
peace, and a people who prosper. I am a man of war—raised on it
as a child teethes on a biscuit. To hide this truth, I have surrounded
myself with many excellent advisers, and I willed myself to accept
their counsel on all matters pertaining to the state and civil counsel.
I need no one to tell me how to spill blood. I need them to tell me
how to make peace. But I grow restless listening to their counsel, for
I have no instincts about the laws for a gentle life, a quiet kingdom.
So you must know me, know this conflict in my heart. I am a man
of war given a kingdom ready for peace. I feign interest when my
counselors speak but cannot drag my heart back from the battlefield.
I cannot change the inner man, Esther. I have never tried, until you.
You can make me become the man of peace I need to be. You can
make me fit to rule a nation, not just conquer it. Kiss me and impart
the wisdom of your words. Lie down with me and teach me what it
is to love."

He began kissing my neck softly and stroking my hair. Then he
moved in front of me and, as he spoke, fell to one knee. "Make me
the man that the court poets say I am. Make me worthy of this crown
I wear. Make me, my Star, worthy of you."

In that moment, diary, I began to love. The heart that would not
be forced seemed to go willingly now. Xerxes is a good man, and he
will be great. Now I, too, have begun to dream of this empire and
what can be.

Tomorrow night we will attend a royal exhibition for all the
peoples of the empire. Xerxes' most valiant warriors will fight against
one another and terrible beasts. I am told the silent and swift warriors

from the East are favored to win, although the mighty ones from our own region are heavily armored. We will see. As a special gift, Xerxes has allowed me to choose a eunuch from his own staff to attend me here in the palace. I have, of course, claimed Hagai. I can do no better than to surround myself with the trusted ones who helped me attain the crown.

With that, I will leave you. Xerxes, being attended to even now, will soon be ready to attend the midnight feast. (How I came to be ready first is a matter of humor to me, for he has switched robes several times now, searching for the robe that will accentuate his crown and thick gold neck chains.) I will emerge soon, with the king on my arm, and attend the feast I was denied as a girl under Mordecai's charge.

35

Sixth Day of Month of Adar
Eighth Year of the Reign of Xerxes
Year 3399 after Creation

I don't know where to start.

Life can change so fast. Lightning can destroy in an instant, but it also illuminates.

It felt so good to be back among the people. I wanted to inhale their scents, memorize every face, and touch them somehow, to carry part of them back with me to my confining quarters. But I was in the royal seating box next to the seat of Xerxes. His royal seat was surrounded by the officers of the court, with Prime Minister Haman on his left and the nobles of each province in the rows beneath our feet. Haman stood to welcome the people, and to queue the musicians for a most majestic greeting of King Xerxes.

Acrobats came leaping and tumbling out of the stadium doors, followed by young girls tossing flowers on the ground, a carpet of petals for Xerxes to tread. I couldn't help but wonder if these young girls were the newest arrivals to his harem. But then the Immortals came through the doors, and they are a sight that can make one cold even in the noonday sun. Their helmets of bronze cast strange shadows across their eyes. Their enormous shields are as tall as their shoulders, and their spears are as ornate as any woman's jewelry. Most feature the sign of the double lion's head, or dragon's horns curling upon themselves. The Immortals also wear richly orna-mented robes. (How easy it must have been to distinguish between warriors during the battles with Greece—Mordecai once told me the Greek men often fight nude!) The crowd grew quiet, and for a moment, all I could hear were the heavy treads of an army. The last man entered now, leading a camel to the center of the stadium. I was confused for a moment why such a beast would be brought. Surely no one would fight the plodding creature.

An Immortal stepped forward and gave a command, and the beast knelt. The men circled around it, and slit its throat. Red blood spurted into the air against the blue Persian sky. Each Immortal stepped forward and dipped his sword in the blood, raising it high above his head, before running to a place along the wall of the sta-dium as the poor animal's body was dragged away. The men were lining the walls, each ready to fight or, if not called, ready to ensure the other warriors fought to the death.

Then Xerxes entered, being drawn in a gold chariot, looking radiant in his crown and robes. The people screamed for him, and he tossed gold coins in high arcs in every direction. While Xerxes was circling the stadium, enjoying the crowd, I noticed the young girls giggling and pointing shyly to Haman near me. It was true, Haman was as handsome as the palace rumors had led us all to believe. I tried to smile at the girls, remembering their age of innocence. Haman, for his part, seemed to enjoy the flattery, though he did not outwardly

acknowledge the girls. He merely sat a bit taller when they were stealing glances at him!

When Xerxes was done showering the people closest to us with
coins, he sat, a signal that the games could now begin. His seating
box offered the best view of the warriors, and it offered the people
the best view of me, but I was still isolated from them. It did me such
good to be so near Mordecai. Oh, I knew he was there, although I
couldn't see him. I knew the laughs and cheers that carried to my ears
carried the sound of his voice as well, and I felt as if the sun was again
shining on me through the heavy weight of the crown.

I wore my hair loose for the exhibition, and I could tell that King
Xerxes approved. My dress was lower than I would have liked, revealing more bosom than proper for the masses and the daytime, but I
knew I was meant to outshine Vashti. It is wearying to be the second
queen. I know the people see three people when they look on the king
and me, for they are comparing me always to Vashti.

Every warrior presented himself to us both, bowing low and
shouting allegiance to the king. One by one, they were led out
and presented, rows of mighty men. The cheering grew louder
as the army grew larger. The crowd was bloodthirsty, but they
loved their men. The warriors from the East were as mysterious, and
controlled, as I could have imagined. They wore no heavy armor,
but seemed as confident as the men brandishing swords. Even I was
anxious to see them fight. I was getting swept away with the crowd,
and I couldn't conceal a broad smile when Xerxes stroked my neck.
Perhaps I was learning to make my final peace now with this crown on
my head, and my new life with this man at my side. Or perhaps it just
felt good to have the wind blowing on my face, unfettered by palace

walls, and to be only one of many under the Persian sun. The harem had made me too rare a creature.

But who would cut a child down as it took its first step? For that is what happened next. The warriors from the winter region, Susa, were led out, and there he was. The two years apart had served him well; perhaps it was his own heartache that had etched the muscles so deeply across his chest. His hair was darker, and he was taller and more dangerous than I remembered, but it was him. It all came back to me now at once, forcing my breath out and stopping my heart. The mountainside, his touch and kiss, his smell, his skin, his smile. Suddenly Xerxes's hand on my neck felt like a limp fish, and I recoiled from my very clothes, this ornate robe and crown, and this man who had stolen my life from me. Would that I could have grabbed Cyrus's sword and struck Xerxes down just then!

Cyrus bowed low but held my eyes, even as he shouted his allegiance to Xerxes. Hagai was seated just to my left, at my feet, and he must have sensed who this man was. I could feel Hagai's eyes on me, willing me to hold steady and reveal nothing. The battles began, and as if far away, I could hear the crowd's roar. I knew the fights were worthy of the attention of a kingdom. But I could not concentrate. I was sick, sick as I stared at the back of the man I loved, as he sat in the stands below me, waiting to fight. I leaned into Xerxes not out of affection but sheer weakness. I feared I could faint at any moment. Xerxes relished this show of weak adoration and stroked my hair. He was touching a dead woman.

I willed myself to straighten as Cyrus took the field.

"What is your good pleasure, my king?" he shouted above the crowd.

The king chose the opponent, for his entertainment.

Xerxes turned to me and asked, "What shall it be, my good queen? Who, or what, would you see this good man fight?"

All eyes were on me, and I stared helplessly at Cyrus. He stared solemnly back and bowed. I could not know what he was thinking. My mind tried to work, but it was like turning over heavy stones after a rainfall. I would not have Cyrus fight a man, for this man next to me had already defeated him. I would choose an animal, and I could only remember, in flashes, that night on the mountain, when we fought a great monster together.

"He will fight a lion," was my quiet command. Xerxes echoed it to the gamekeepers, and they loosed a great beast onto the field. The crowd roared its pleasure to me.

Cyrus wasted no time considering the irony; his sword was out of its sheath in a blinding moment, and he held the lion at bay as it circled him, snarling. I could not watch and buried my face in Xerxes' robe. It was awful, for everything I was doing only fed Xerxes' misguided notion that I was his, body and soul.

Xerxes tried to bolster my courage. "Look up, my pet! Would you miss the fight?"

I watched, for Xerxes' benefit, but could only avert my eyes when the lion would lunge and swing his massive paws. Cyrus was smooth and measured, and stayed out of the lion's reach, sometimes using his shield to force a glare into the lion's eyes as it lunged. Heavy blows of the claws were met with Cyrus's shield, and all of Cyrus's attempts to undercut the lion's belly were futile. I remembered how we had defeated the mountain lion together. Cyrus had not escaped without my help that night, and I knew no way to save him now, though my mind flew in all directions to find one.

The lion seemed to slow, and Cyrus lowered his shield a moment to wipe sweat from his brow, stopping it from running into his eyes. The shield looked to weigh as much as I, and I wondered if Cyrus was slowing, too, in the sun. At that instant the lion opened its mouth, panting, but a subtle tensing of its muscles alarmed me. It lunged, and lunged low, ripping open the flesh of Cyrus's calf. Cyrus screamed and reached for the bleeding wound, and the lion struck again. But Cyrus became as an animal himself and drew a knife from a belt around his other calf. Ducking his head as he bent forward to receive the lion's blow, Cyrus ran his blade into the beast as it snarled in pain, its blood spilling onto the ground with Cyrus's. He had stabbed it in the heart, piercing it on the diagonal from chest to arm. Blood was spurting in high arcs above both heads. The knife remained in the beast, and Cyrus drew his sword now, leaving the shield on the ground. The lion staggered, and Cyrus drove the giant sword straight down, severing the spine. The lion fell at an odd angle, like a child's doll. Cyrus had to brace a foot against the monster to jerk his sword free, and the beast remained still.

The crowd was silent for a moment, staring at the fallen beast, and then lifted Cyrus's name in a fierce chant. All the other warriors lifted their weapons high in the air, saluting their brother as other beasts screamed from their cages below, smelling blood. Cyrus had granted us a marvelous opening, and several warriors, emboldened by his success, would now die imitating him.

Xerxes turned to me, alive with excitement. "What a show, my dear! How will we reward this warrior for the excellent entertainment?"

I could only shake my head, dumb and mute. The king grew immediately concerned, for my appearance must have been as ill as

I felt. "What is it, good queen?" he whispered urgently to me. "You look unwell."

I was so weakened by shock, by the ghost of my past, that my newest secret spilled out too easily. "I am with child, my lord," I replied softly, the sweat breaking out on my brow and lips unbidden.

Xerxes threw back his head and laughed, drawing me close to his side. Then he stood and addressed his kingdom. "This has been a day that will live on in the hearts of Persians forever! A new champion, and a new heir!" He raised a goblet to toast the stadium, and the people roared.

Xerxes toasted again, this time tipping his cup toward Cyrus. "Well done, mighty Cyrus! Come forward and greet your king!" As Cyrus moved toward us, a boy ran forward to wipe his sword clean of blood.

Cyrus bowed, presenting his sword once to the king, and then to the crowd, before sheathing it. Xerxes motioned to me, as if presenting me to Cyrus, and Cyrus took my hand in his, kissing it once, tenderly. It was a stolen kiss, because I wanted him here alone, without the crowd and this king, and he let me taste this dream but not enter it. Then Cyrus turned and faced Xerxes, who was by now quite red from excitement and too much wine.

"For your bravery here tonight, Cyrus, you will be rewarded!" The crowd cheered Xerxes' words. "Honorable Cyrus, you will take command of the palace guard, and protect the crown from every threat! You will be the most revered warrior in the kingdom! Honor to Cyrus!"

"Honor to Cyrus! And long life to our king!" shrieked the crowd.

Their chants ringing in my ears, I was led back to the king's chambers, where I attended him with a dull and aching heart.

36

Third Day of Nisan
Ninth Year of the Reign of Xerxes
Year 3400 after Creation

It is now the third day of the new year, and only days ago I saw Cyrus. I feel so weak right now, and my stomach rolls at the sight of food. I do not know if I am heartsick, or if the pregnancy affects me so strongly. My head swims if I think too long on that day. I try to lie still and imagine that I am lying in a field of flowers, their soft petals my blankets. There is no breeze to ruffle me, only a warm sun and the sound of a river. I try so hard to push all away.

But a knock on my door this morning brought me awake. "Enter," I commanded, and was met with the sight of many men. After the harem year, I should be comfortable with men seeing me not properly dressed, but I quickly draped a robe around my shoulders as I sat up in bed. My breakfast, untasted, was on a low table near me. I had not heard the servant bring it.

The littlest one, a man with a face like a walnut, brown from the sun and shriveled, bowed in an elaborate fashion. "Greetings to the queen on behalf of the gods," he said, his voice very sharp and crisp. It did not set well on my stomach. He clapped and the men stumbled forward and dispersed from behind him, fanning out until I saw all their ranks. It looked as if Xerxes has assembled a man from every region. Each was dressed differently, each man wearing his hair differently, or bundled under a wrap. One carried a dead rabbit by its hind legs. Another held an enormous bouquet of lavender blossoms. (Lovely as they were, their smell mixed with the sweat of these men made my head spin.) Several held bags of fur, with untold horrors inside.

"We have been sent on Xerxes' good wishes to see how the queen would be attended to in her pregnancy," the little man said. "Whatever god you serve, we stand ready to perform a blessing."

I stared at him, unable to take in the sight and think quickly of a lie.

The old man saw my hesitation and raised his hands in front of his face eagerly, as if he was patting the air. "Of course, of course," he said. "How wise you are, how wise and how beautiful!" he added, bowing low again. I was afraid I would throw up, but there was no bowl near me. I took a deep breath, which I held in.

"You do not wish to claim allegiance to one god in a land of so many," he said. "Ahura Mazda be praised! The Great Lord of the underworld sees your kindness toward all true believers who worship him in all his forms. Grace to you, majesty!"

Once again, my stomach rolled over and I madly waved him toward the door, another hand over my mouth.

"Very well! Let us exit, my friends!" he exclaimed, herding them all through the door at once.

I wonder, will I conduct all matters of state with such grace?

37

Twenty-fourth Day of the Month of Sivan
Ninth Year of the Reign of Xerxes
Year 3400 after Creation

So much has been written in these pages; I suppose my doom is assured if it is discovered. So there can be no further harm in revealing more. What alarms me most truly is the dark side of the gift in my womb that G-d has granted Xerxes, for now there are more people who might want to kill me, and more reason to do so. As I draw closer to Xerxes, I may also draw closer to the blades drawn and waiting for a taste of my neck. But let me tell you now of why my fear blossoms:

This morning, as I rose from my bed and was attended to in my bath, I had the strangest sensation of being watched. I had grown so accustomed to bathing on the roof in the harem, that I had requested of Xerxes to construct a similar bath on the roof of the queen's palace as well. It has taken his laborers almost a year to dig the channels and create a garden all around for me, but I do love it. It is, quite truly, an oasis of escape for me in these walls. I have even taken to the custom of bathing in the morning, when the sun is coolest, and the water most refreshing, as opposed to the other women who still observe the local custom of bathing at night. Perhaps that is why I had such a strange sensation today; this feeling of being exposed, but then, this has been my practice for so long, why would it seem wrong today? No, I am sure I was being watched, although I do not know by whom, or why.

Now even more than before, I am careful to stay secluded, with only my trusted advisers from the harem near me. My food is tasted twice over, my wine from a private reserve that Hagai and another eunuch from the court keep watch over. When I sleep there are always two or more awake at my side.

I asked G-d for this child to ease my aching heart; how is it now that my heart is burdened as never before? What cruel justice is this? I know I cannot keep myself safe, nor this child inside of me. I took no care for myself in the past. But my life is all that will protect the child, even as the child puts my life at risk.

And yet I love this child already as I have never loved. I suspect this will have my secret out, but I am not afraid somehow. I will tell this child of our G-d, I will bring my little one to the rabbi for a blessing. I may soon at last be able to bring Mordecai to me, and how happy a reunion we will have! In all of my daydreaming, I find that one hand always goes to stroke my belly. It has begun to swell and I am in my fourth month, according to the physician. (I have asked to be attended to by the palace physician. He is a man of no particular persuasion in worship; he aspires only to worship science. Having attended the royals, he has seen much and will keep me in good health. I am forlorn not to have a Jewish sister attend me, but to ask for one of the midwives from the village is to risk revealing myself.)

I have asked Hagai to keep careful watch down below from my chamber window, and Ashtari to cover my body more completely with linens as I emerge from the waters.[1]

---

1 See corresponding commentary on page 283 of the appendix.

38

Seventh Day of the Month of Tammuz
Ninth Year of the Reign of Xerxes
Year 3400 after Creation

Blood was spilled today, but it was not my own, although it was of my body, for Xerxes' heir has died in my womb. I was eating dinner, the nausea finally having departed this week, when the hair on the back of my neck stood up. It was as if I felt a great storm coming. I pushed my plate away and paced in my chambers. At first, when I saw the blood, I did not comprehend, but the mother wisdom of my spirit, my bones, knew before my brain and perhaps even my heart. All was lost.

The pain was unbearable, and I clenched a strip of cloth between my teeth as waves of pain came over me, wrenching away this life little by little. I wept so bitterly, my breath coming in gasps between each jolt of agony. I did not get to say good-bye. I feel I've lost the best friend, the deepest love, ever granted me, before I ever got to know the face, or hear the beloved's voice. It is a grief I cannot explain.

There is a sadness more final than I have ever known; the world seems dulled over with a wash of gray. I once feared the enemy beyond my chambers. I did not know my own womb could betray me. She is an evil, double-minded sister. My heart is so raw and bruised I cannot bear even the musicians to come near my window. All I long to do is lie silently, as the life ebbs away from within and I am left alone.

I was a fool to feel so happy with this life inside. I was a fool to believe G-d would ever grant me relief in this palace that has set its face against Him with its pagan worship and unrestrained lusts. If I have not brought this upon myself, then they have brought it upon us all.

Only Ashtari can soothe me, and she remembers the words of the shepherd king David that I have quoted to her, "Do not be sad, little heart, for you will again have reason to praise your G-d." She brings me fresh cotton to stop the flow of blood and crushes herbs into oil for me to eat with my bread.

Xerxes took the news with only a fleeting grief; he is busy with a kingdom and has many heirs by other women. Perhaps he is glad to have my body back as his alone. He has had many women and taken from them as he desired. It does not seem strange to him that nature should take what she wanted too.

How I long now for a word from Mordecai. I will send him a message tonight and wait for a reply. A word of comfort from home would do me much good.

39

The days that have passed have eased my pain, and I am able to draw strength from the many who love me here. I avert my eyes, and heart, when I pass those who might celebrate such a wretched thing. The other wives must pity me, and perhaps be jealous of me, but they will not again fear me. A queen without children is only a wife who wears the crown. True power belongs to the one who raises the king's heir.

The crown was coveted by the harem girls because of the great wealth of the king; the wise wives have known all along that wealth is less pleasurable over a lifetime than power. This, then, is my small comfort, the irony I see: If palace intrigue claims my life, it will not be at the hands of a mother positioning her son ahead of mine. This little death might have perhaps saved me from my own.

Another strange thing; there was a single red rose on my bed tonight when I retired to my chambers. I do not think that it is from Xerxes. King Xerxes has been away from me several nights now. He is still celebrating our marriage with a feast, Esther's Feast, he calls it. He has handed out generous gifts to everyone in the kingdom. (I wonder what Mordecai received! And to think they have no idea he is my adopted father! I must suppose he received a trinket like everyone else.) Here I sit, in my royal palace, unable to attend the festivities. It is not good for me to have so much time to think. My royal chamber seems more like a prison cell with every hour. My mind escapes to fantasy over and over and grows more reluctant to return. The irony of Cyrus guarding me in this palace! I do not see him, but I know he is nearby, keeping me safe for the king, knowing all the while I am stolen property, that I once belonged to him.

I could read nothing in his face at the fight in the stadium. I do not know him anymore; that is a truth I must face. Does he relish being near, knowing he can never again touch? Or perhaps he has forgotten me altogether and married one of the girls that his father prescribed? There is another sickening possibility, but I cannot believe it of Cyrus: There are those who adore the crown more than the head that wears it. Perhaps Cyrus has followed in his father's footsteps, and longs to be near me only to use me for gain. I have been absent from him, from home, for almost three years, and I can no longer be sure he has not changed. My emotions swing wildly from wanting to see him, to dreading what I will find. Does he hate me? Does he even know it was his own father who sent me here, against my will? I am a prisoner, surely he knows that, when he himself is now the jailer! What girl would choose to live this life, a delicately groomed little pet, allowed out of its cage only at the whim of the master?

I do expect Xerxes to call me to his chambers when he is high from wine, or tired of the girls from the harem. But it would be unthinkable for me to attend the feast in the presence of common men. I know Xerxes will not repeat his humiliation with Vashti. I can only imagine how much the girls of the harem are enjoying him in my absence. I am not alone, however, in my plight—every woman in the kingdom understands how I feel, for when a woman hosts a feast for her husband, she must prepare the food and then retreat to an upstairs room, never to be seen during the party. Does a jewel become more rare if it never sees the light of day? I suppose it must in the men's eyes. I can only pace restlessly in my palace, and pray and plead with G-d to have mercy on the women of Athens. News has reached me that they now ask for democracy themselves. The people here watch Greece closely.

The prostitutes of Athens are foreign women who do not proscribe to such treatment as our own cloistering and seclusion; they are unafraid to bare their faces to the sun and greet a man openly. And so the men, who bought these women to forget their troubles, are getting more trouble than they ever could have wished for. How ironic that the prostitutes brought about the chance of freedom for the wives! I never cease to be amazed at how G-d will use everything, even evil, to work for good. The Athenian women had no choice but to let their husbands indulge in unclean living; now their freedom is being slowly bought with money meant for harlots.

But of course, I will not see that freedom in these lands in my lifetime. I know that. It is enough, I believe, to know that a candle has been lit in the shadows. I will trust that G-d will still be at work long after I am gone, and that these later women will know how best to use their freedom.

40

Fourth Day of the Month of Adar
Eleventh Year of the Reign of Xerxes
Year 3403 after Creation[1]

This is the month of good fortune, and what fortune we have had! My hands find it hard to write steadily when I review the events of today, though the king kissed them repeatedly and told me not to fear. I have just delivered a message to the king, from Mordecai, that two of the palace eunuchs, Bigthana and Teresh, who guard the King's Gate, have plotted to kill him. Mordecai delivered the message to me by my servant Stateira, who received it from the eunuch she sent to buy red roses for me.

I felt sick when I read Mordecai's note. Bigthana and Teresh are highly trusted, and highly visible. If they have plotted this evil, what else could be lurking in the palace? I have been here over four years

---

1 There are gaps in the diary entries that appear to be unaccounted for. Experts speculate that there are two plausible reasons for the missing dates: theft (by ancient or modern tomb raiders), or that Esther was inattentive to her diaries at times. Because Queen Esther's diaries were offered for sale by a private party, who would not disclose the circumstances in which they had been acquired, forensic scientists have had difficulties exploring these theories. Later in the diaries, where the most obvious gaps appear, we will revisit these explanations.

now, and I have seen many petty squabbles, especially among the advisers to the king, but this shocked me deeply. My mind races ahead and I imagine bloodshed and falling to the sword myself if an enemy disposes of Xerxes. Xerxes has been my captor, but he is also now my shield. I wondered why Mordecai had not simply alerted Haman, the king's most trusted servant, who often attends to matters at the King's Gate. Mordecai has written to me that everyone bows to this man and pays deepest homage and respect to him. Haman continually finds favor with his counsel to the king. Why did Haman, then, not know of this plot? Haman knows all that occurs within the king's gates. Either he has misjudged the loyalty of these two men, or is himself misjudged as a worthy adviser. I feel dread when I think of how close evil sleeps to the king, and so to me. How many others would kill him, kill us, and will they be unmasked in time? How odd it is to see my twentieth birthday, and count myself fortunate for it!

But back to the more urgent horror Mordecai had written about. As G-d would have it, after I received the note, Xerxes called me to his chambers at once. The message from Mordecai burned in my hand. How would I explain it? How did a queen come into possession of a note from a male commoner? Everyone knew why I was being called; but no one knew why my feet flew so quickly down the corridor to his bedchamber. I drew a deep breath as the doors were opened for me. Xerxes knew at once I was not right. He removed my veil[2] softly and led me to a chair. I found I could not speak, but instead handed him the note.

---

2 At this time in the history of Iran, before the birth of the Islamic faith, only married women in the Middle East wore veils, intended as a sign of highest honor. Anyone else caught wearing a veil would be beaten.

His face grew hard as he read the lines, and he turned and summoned his guards, whispering a command. The guards' grips tightened around their swords, and they left to fulfill the king's wishes.

Xerxes turned back to me and smiled. As I have often told you, he is not a man of details. He asked no questions about Mordecai or the note. Instead he drew me into his arms and began to wash my distress away with his kisses. He had not called me to his chambers to be distracted with a plot of unhappy palace guards; my lion had only grown hungry for me. I sighed and settled into his embrace. Perhaps it will afford me the chance to bear a child. There are times, I confess, that I find myself welcoming his touch only for the dream of having a child.

Yes, as I write it now, this story of my days, like all the days following my coronation, seems to me now to be a disappointment. For all my excitement and adventures, I am still a royal prisoner. I know I will never be returned to my people, or Mordecai, or to my dreams of Cyrus, and I still cannot reveal my secret. My role as Xerxes' queen means I am little more than plumage for his kingdom, and I wonder if this is how I will fill all my years. If I am not to be a mother, what will sustain me? How will I spend my time in this palace? Is this all G-d has called me to? Why, oh Lord, have you endowed me with such qualities that will never be used in my situation? Why have you given me a desire for more, when I know it can never be? There was a time when I wanted to be queen, for it seemed a way out. But now I want more. Curse this heart that stays awake when life all around has fallen asleep.

To see the spring lambs and tend my roses, to feel the warm sand under my toes and on my face, to grow sleepy in the noonday heat. These little freedoms of the people, those I miss and imagine they could comfort me in ways that gold and jewels cannot. But I must be grateful. Ashtari says discontent shows in a woman's features, making her undesirable to a man. So I will be grateful that I still have the king's heart—although I must share his body—and grateful for my crown. I may long to set eyes on dear Mordecai, but I will be grateful for the continual counsel through his notes sent to me in secret by his friends at the palace gates. I long, too, to walk freely through the streets of Susa, but inside the palace I am freely given all I ask. This is not such an unpleasant ending for an orphan, and I will resolve to honor G-d with my portions. Yes, this is a feast I have been given, and it is wrong of me to dream of the crumbs of freedom I once had. Do not let me betray my king, or my G-d, with thoughts of the happy past. Let those be forever sealed and lost, for they belonged to a daughter named Hadassah, who walked among the Jews of Susa. She is no more.

Yet one small burning ember remains of her, and would that I could quench it! For as long as I know Cyrus is outside my gates, I cannot give all of myself to the king. My heart betrays me in my weak moments, and I see myself in Cyrus's arms. I hate him for it at times. I must be free to love my king. (I wonder so often what is the nature of love—is it a decision made on earth, of logic and reason, a choice made in the time here between dust and dust? Is it made in heaven, a supernatural force that binds us together in this world, and the next? Is love made in man's will, or G-d's heart?)

One of my servants told me this as she brushed my hair: "We each have many lives, lived in succession. We love in another life the one denied to us in this one." She seemed so sure, although no one she knows has ever returned from the dead to confirm her theory, and it seems to me only an excuse. I know she is in love with a kitchen servant she cannot have (his wife and three children being lively obstacles) and the hallway guard would have her for himself. I suspect he has plied her with this promise she can love another later!

G-d help me, I do not always want to turn my thoughts away from Cyrus, but I know I cannot have what I want. Why should I live a half-life, torn from a memory of a boy who has grown into a man; and who is to say I could have ever loved the man? I belong to the king, the man who made me what I am.

This is why they never spoke of love in the harem. For who can teach the heart? I can pose my arms just so, I can cast down my eyes, and roll my hips; I can seduce, but I cannot control whom I love. The physical arts are just a masquerade, and these jesters pray no one removes their secret, innermost veils, or the deception is lost. Yes, every girl who goes into the king is an amusement, and nothing more, meant for him the way you would amuse a baby by some shining scrap.

The king has given his heart to me, however—and a wretched recipient I am if I will not return it fully. I lie awake night after night, reasoning with my heart, the way a farmer pleads for rain. How is it women learn to master their hearts? Is it effortless for some, and they are allowed to marry and be content? Have there been others, like me, who went to the altar with a cleaved heart? How did they learn to love—or forget—fully? It is not enough to persuade my heart that I have to keep offering my body night after night, no matter who my heart loves. I give myself willingly, but then close my eyes to sleep, and in my dreams all is undone. I am again with Cyrus.

41

Eighth Day of the Month of Nisan
Eleventh Year of the Reign of Xerxes
Year 3403 after Creation

Ashtari was angry with me when I awoke this morning. She had not slept in my chambers but in her own bed, some distance down the corridor of the palace. She shoved something onto my lap as I struggled to adjust my eyes to the morning light.

"I know of the rose that was left for you. I would have thought nothing of it, save that this was beside your bed when I entered this morning. This is the gift of a suitor." Her tone was accusing.

I looked closely at what she had shoved toward me. It was a pouch made from the hide of an animal, perhaps one of the minks that the men in the eastern portion of the empire raise. It was heavy, and as I opened the drawstring, a rope of jewels slid out into my hand. It had a thick cluster of sapphires in the center, with sapphires dangling from many loops on either side of the cluster, all the way around the necklace. I was speechless, and for Ashtari, this was just as damning. She glared at me until I found my tongue.

"Ashtari, why do you accuse me of betrayal? I have done nothing wrong, and you know this."

"Who is leaving you these gifts?" she demanded.

"I do not know, and even if I did, what could I do? I am attended by you and the servants faithfully; I am never out of your sight, save for my evenings in the king's bed. Yes, that is the only time I am away from here, and would you accuse me of cheating even there?"

Her face softened as she knew I was right. I had done nothing wrong that she could see, and yet she was uneasy.

"It is all too easy for a queen to die, Esther. Perhaps you have done nothing, perhaps you have cast a glance to someone who mistook your meaning. I do not know, but I know others have been killed for less than this. Do I remind you that if you die, I will die as well? You were brought here a prisoner some five years ago; do you forget I have been held here much longer? Yet you do not see me behaving recklessly. I content myself to live in your shadow, even as you live in the king's. But this lovely necklace may well cost all of us our necks."

I was at a loss, for I had not invited these gifts, nor did I know whom they came from. I could not be sure they were not from Xerxes, but I could not ask him, either.

"Do nothing, Ashtari. We must wait, wait for someone to tip his hand." I eyed her coldly for a moment so she would not miss my next point. "Never question my loyalty again, Ashtari. I am loyal to the crown, and to the king, and I am loyal to a G-d you know nothing of. I would sooner die than betray this G-d, or my king." I softened my words now with a smile and reached for her hand. "Or my closest friend."

42

Fourth Day of the Month of Iyyar
Eleventh Year of the Reign of Xerxes
Year 3403 after Creation

The last few days have passed quietly. Ashtari and Hagai stay alert, but my suitor has not revealed himself, if he be not Xerxes, nor has he sent any more gifts to me in the dark of night. It may well have been Xerxes himself, for he is prone to sending gifts unannounced and for no reason. We shall see.

As I wait for the truth to be revealed, Xerxes has given the order for everyone at the King's Gate to bow down when Haman passes, and Mordecai refuses to do so. Haman has continued to climb through the ranks of Xerxes' trusted advisers, until there is no one who has the king's ear more readily, save for myself. I have never met him, although he was present at my coronation, I am sure, and of course at the great exhibition that followed. I would like to meet him, though, if it were ever possible, as Hagai tells me no one is more clever, or protective of the king and his interests, than this Haman. The king honors him. The exterior guards have been beseeching Mordecai, whom they've become accustomed to seeing every day at the palace gates, to bow down like the rest of them when Haman arrives and is announced. Yet Mordecai refuses to bow because Haman is an Agagite, and Haman's pride is wounded.

How my thoughts of Mordecai make me smile as I write this! I know it is not pride that keeps him standing but his love of our Lord. "How can you bow down to a man, when your people have seen the glory of the Lord?" he would often ask me when we saw others practicing their strange customs. "G-d has left us no room for the awe of man." What I loved best about Mordecai was that he loved so many people so well. In some people, love of G-d leaves little love for others, especially those who stumble and sin often. But Mordecai loved G-d so well that his love was multiplied, and all felt at ease in his presence. I am ashamed to say I pitied myself as a young girl; now I wonder if others envied me, that I was raised in a home of such love.

I never told this to my good cousin, but during the festival days of our people, when we would make our long walk to hear instruction and praises from our holy men, those were the days I treasured most. Yes, I complained of blisters on my feet, and of the sun, and of the way our lunch smelled in its goatskin bag. But at Mordecai's side, his hand in mine, he taught me of life and G-d and all things worth living for. He loved to quote Solomon, "Even in laughter the heart may ache." He wanted me to see so much more than what met my eyes. He taught me to look for the sadness in the eyes of the widows at market, the exhaustion behind the smile of a woman when her time to birth is close at hand. No wonder he was the most beloved of our village.

Haman knows Mordecai not. Would that Haman could draw

closer and see Mordecai for who he is! For I know Mordecai does not oppose Haman, but merely stands for what he knows to be true. I pray all this will be settled in good time.

43

Tenth Day of the Month of Elul
Eleventh Year of the Reign of Xerxes
Year 3403 after Creation

The courts are quiet this evening, and likely will be for several more days. The Magi have arrived to give blessings and prophecies from Ahura Mazda. Xerxes and I have talked long of religion and gods; I could not reveal my secret, that I am a Jew, but I did express my disdain and weariness of so many secret idols in the land and the courts. The false teachers create discord among sisters and friends, and have introduced so many girls to opium and dishonor. Mordecai tells me that in some idol temples, a bride must give herself to a complete stranger before she can return to her groom on their wedding night. It sickens me. Why are people so easily led astray? It is not good for them, and not good for the kingdom.

Xerxes' father, Darius, allowed all to live as they saw fit; Darius even honored our G-d as the one true G-d. But Xerxes, perhaps seeing my point so clearly as he stamped out rebellion from the more volatile sects, has issued a demand that no god is to be publicly worshipped but Ahura Mazda. It is not quite the desired outcome

I would have wished for, and now even I secretly live in rebellion to the crown. I continue to pray daily, facing Jerusalem, reciting what Scriptures are in my memory. I have sent gold to Mordecai to buy sacrifices for me at the appointed times, to intercede for me here, and for our people living under Xerxes' hand.

I am comforted by the story of another Jew who walked these palace halls, also brought here a slave. His name was Daniel, and he was troubled by many restless dreams. How I feel he is my brother now, watching from heaven. He slept, but was disturbed by G-d's hand. I cannot sleep, for fear of being disturbed by the hand of a mortal.

In his dreams, Daniel saw the future, the future of the crown and the empire, and I wonder if he saw me. He prayed in privacy, as I must, even as he knew his enemies were stalking him, wanting to expose his secret and thus end his life.

I am weary of so much deception. Daniel's prophecies were great and many, but as for me, my mind strains to find a reason G-d would keep me here.

44

Twenty-first Day of the Month of Elul
Eleventh Year of the Reign of Xerxes
Year 3403 after Creation

The courts have been quiet for days now, and I have grown accustomed to taking walks through the gardens, unescorted. The Gardens of the Queen are magnificent, each woman before me having left something of herself. Flowers and fruits from every region are here, some bearing one woman's favorite fruit, another a scented blossom that was often tucked behind another's ear. It is enchanting to walk through the rows, and I have selected a spot for my own name, and will, of course, plant a red rosebush. The gardeners have arranged all the trees and plants in such pleasing fashions; some of the greens, which have no fruit or flower and would be cut down in another garden, are instead coaxed into high shapes, and trimmed to resemble animals. (Never was a camel so pleasant to sit under!) Although it is walled in on all four sides, the open sky above brings fresh air, and rain, and the stars seem like blossoms set on high above the trees.

It is a blessed relief to be gone from prying eyes, eyes that admired my robes, or fancied themselves wearing them if the tides of fortune turn inside the palace for some unseen traitor. In the gardens at night, I am again returned to myself, and I smell the flowers, stroking their cool, soft petals, whispering my secrets to them and listening to theirs. Some of the imported flowers do not flourish here, and I endeavor to understand why. I have given notes to the gardener each morning, and look forward all day to returning to my little friends to see how they fare. The pomegranates have been doing so well this year, and a new variety of honeysuckle has made the garden irresistible. Birds of many colors and songs have made their home here with us also. My garden is indeed another country. It is here that I am truly the queen, and I rule with a gentle hand. It is a place of beauty and simple joys, where I can easily uproot what is unpleasant, what does not belong.

On certain rare nights, I am told, a mysterious flower blooms along the east wall. The eunuchs say it is called the Scent of the Beloved, and when it blooms, the dreams of all who smell its fragrance are blessed. Young girls are said to see the faces of their future husbands in their dreams. Old women are said to see the faces of their grandchildren not yet born. I do not know what I would see in my dreams.

I love the garden, too, because it is easier to think of the palace and its events when I am outside of it, rather than in its belly. The garden worked its magic over my time here; the shock I once felt at seeing Cyrus again and having him near (if still unseen), and the mystery of the gifts left to me have faded now in my mind, if that is a blessing. But if I am grateful for the peace in my heart, I am also sorry, for those intrigues had once again stirred my imagination. I felt alive again, in the strange way that only danger and love can give you. Until then, I had almost forgotten the allure of dark discoveries and forbidden dreams. Once remembered, I now force myself to return to my quiet life, my prayers and the garden, and be grateful for the brief distraction that quickened my pulse while my days draw slowly past.

45

Nineteenth Day of the Month of Tishri
Eleventh Year of the Reign of Xerxes
Year 3403 after Creation

I am not sure I will write much more in these pages, nor am I sure what will become of these scrolls when I am gone. As heaven is my witness, I have brought none of this upon myself, but I fear I will die for the transgression just the same.

Tonight as I took my customary stroll through the quiet palace gardens, I again felt another's eyes upon me. I was alone, of course, and my attendants were in the portico, enjoying the wine and night music flowing from the king's palace as the Magi continued to hold sway over the court. Yet I was sure someone was there with me. I should have left. I am cursed that I did not listen to my spirit and flee!

As I moved through the garden, to my favorite retreat of fig trees and rosebushes, where the scents and flavors of creation reach my head faster than spiced wine, a hand reached for me as sudden and darting as a serpent. It wrapped around my mouth so that I could not scream, and the other arm encircled my waist, dragging me to seclusion. I could not see his face, but I felt his breath hot on my neck and saw his drawn dagger flash in his hand. My heart beat so quickly beneath my robe I was sure it would burst forth and fly away from this place. He whispered softly. I strained to recognize his voice. It had been so long ago when I had last heard it like this; would I know his sound now? I tried to remember the touch of his skin, but he had been yet a boy, and time had changed us both.

His whisper was quiet. "How many nights have I longed to hold you in my arms? Do you dream of me, Esther, as I dream of you? For I have watched you moving about in your palace, and these gardens, and I have loved you from a distance for far too long now. My own father married me to a plain and grating woman, whose dowry was to his liking, although he knew the girl was not to mine. I, too, know what it is to suffer, to marry whom you do not love."

These were the words from my own dreams, what I had heard in the shadowlands of sleep, and yet they had no sweetness to them now, spoken like this in Xerxes' garden. I had not expected to hear such bitterness in them. And why would he not let me see his face? He paused for a moment, taking me in with his ragged breaths and rough touch, before continuing:

"I know you cannot have given your heart to a man like Xerxes. He cannot appreciate you the way I can. He was born in the palace and knows nothing else. Only I see the heart you hide within. Only I can love you as the heavens intended. I will not keep you waiting much longer. Soon I will dispose of our enemies, those who would stand before us and our destiny together."

I do not know how, but I found enough voice to reply. "Enemies?"

"Yes, the vile ones who stand in the way of our happiness

together. It will be a tidy business, Esther, and then you will be mine. For now, I can ask only for your trust." He ran the blade of the dagger along one of my arms, and I shivered in the hot desert night air.

"Why must you shed blood if it is only me you want? I am not worth the lives of so many," I said in confusion. This was not the gentle boy I had known; what had happened in the years of my absence? What had Mordecai omitted in his letters? Yet how could I judge what Cyrus had become? I was different, too. I had lain with another man, spent my years making my body his own secret garden. I was no longer a girl who sold fleeces and stole chaste kisses in the moonlight.

He laughed, grabbing my hair and burying his face in it, inhaling deeply. As he exhaled, I could smell the wine from the king's palace.

"Ah. Already you keep pace with me," he remarked. "It is true I want something else. Why go to war, if not for all the spoils? If we are to be lovers, I should tell you everything, should I not? But then, not yet. You will know all in good time."

His blade followed the line of my robe, from the soft of my thigh, to my belly, and between my breasts, as if he would caress me with its blade, and he then laughed. "Mordecai has made it all so easy for me. He got such pleasure in denying me what was due me, and I thought often of merely dragging him into an darkened doorway and slitting his throat in revenge. But thorns lead to roses, do they not? He has unwittingly delivered the crown into my hands, through a people whose riches will finance my campaign. They are an unruly people, dedicated to an invisible god of shadows, and would never see me be king. I have but to destroy them, and plunder their houses, and then the crown will be within my certain grasp. Then you will take your rightful place as well, at the side of a true king, one who rules a kingdom, not one who merely governs it."

He planted a soft kiss on my neck, then released me.

I stumbled forward between the fig trees back onto the path and caught the eye of Ashtari, who had begun to sweep the garden with her eyes to check on me. When she saw me, her brow raised slightly, but I shook my head and pretended to examine whatever blossom was nearest. I tried to catch a glimpse of him as he left, but could not.

I was grateful when they called me in and I retired to my chambers. I should have been flush with pleasure, but dread swam in my stomach, and I felt doubly wretched, for it was only Xerxes' strong hand that I first thought of to steady me.

46

Thirtieth Day of the Month of Kislev
Eleventh Year of the Reign of Xerxes
Year 3403 after Creation

He knows. G-d help me, but he knows. I must love him somewhere in my deepest spirit, I think, for I fear as much for his heartbreak as for my own neck. When I was in his chambers, lying in his arms, he was stroking my hair, and asked me the question I had no answer for.

"Why is it you never say you love me, Esther?" Xerxes whispered in the darkness. The only reply came from the songbird kept in the far corner of the chamber, nearest the window. She sang a sad song tonight, soft and low, and I wondered where her heart was as well.

Xerxes sat up on one elbow and laughed. "The harem girls can't quit saying it when they're brought to my chambers! But you. Not even once."

I tried a joke of my own. "They are mere words. Words as thin as air. They cannot put gold in your treasury or buy silver for your swords. What use has the great Xerxes for words, and words from a woman?"

"If you think so little of them, why will you not share them with me?" he asked, turning somber now. "I am here, in Susa, but you are far away. Where are you, Esther?"

I could not find my voice. I looked away and felt so naked. I tried to cover myself with the bedclothes, but he jerked the sheets away and stared at me fiercely.

"Whose arms are you in tonight? If I could, I would strike him down with my sword before your very eyes! For what king ever had to watch as another man stole the queen from his very bed?"

I felt a tear roll down my hot, shamed cheek, and he looked away, unmoved.

"The first night you came to me here, I swore to you I would not take you against your will. You offered your heart freely for the crown you wear today. I have invaded countries, crossed seas, watched as my men spilled their blood for me on thirsty desert sands. I am a man of war, but for you, I would live as a man of peace. I have commanded a million warriors, Esther; why do I not command your heart?"

I could not answer, and his words went on.

"My thirst to see blood spilled has returned," he threatened. "I will find out who you love, Esther, and destroy him." Xerxes stood over the bed then turned away toward the window.

"My king!" I cried out. "Your guards watch me day and night. I am never alone! You know I have not betrayed you!"

"You have lied to me, Esther!" he screamed as he threw the songbird off the balcony, her cage crashing down the steps into the garden, her frightened cries hurting my ears, for I was next.

"I rule a kingdom of liars!" he yelled at me. "My food is tasted for poison, my wine is strained for shards of glass, my bed stripped to check for asps and adders! I tolerate it all because I have a dream:

a dream for this empire to be ruled by men's minds, never again their swords. I dream of a kingdom where children will once again play in the streets with no fear of the setting sun, and no mother knows the grief of burying a child who was forced to war instead of school. Persia will be a kingdom where the people die full of years and laughter."

His voice now grew quiet as he looked at me. "But it is your dreams that are my undoing, Esther, for I do not know who steals into our bed when your eyes are closed."

He laughed softly and handed me my robes.

"You were right about one thing, my queen. You once told me no other harem girl would love the man, only the crown. You said you were different. How right you were, for you love neither." With this, he banged on the door for the guards, who entered with swords drawn and led me back to my quarters.

47

Twenty-first Day of the Month of Adar
Eleventh Year of the Reign of Xerxes
Year 3403 after Creation

It has now been two full weeks since I was called to Xerxes. I have never been absent from him for so long, save for the royal feasts he must give for the men according to the customs between the king and the people. There is no such event now. I have been abandoned, and perhaps will be forgotten.

I sent a note to Mordecai, warning him of my midnight conversation with Cyrus in the garden, and hastening him to find out all he could, for no one is safe at the moment. I am afraid to stroll in my gardens at night for refuge; I am afraid to bathe without the cover of many attendants. I do not know when Cyrus will unveil his desperate acts, but I know I must have no part in it. I have begged G-d for Cyrus on so many nights, but I know this is not G-d's hand at work. G-d would never violate Himself to give me what I desire, and would I not be receiving Cyrus in dishonor? Xerxes will surely think I had a part in this plan, and thus I am in greater danger. Why, but why is goodness so sparse in this world, and evil only compounded?

To add to my worries, Hagai has received a message from Hathach, the eunuch who often attends the king, that the former queen Vashti and her son, Artaxerxes, are amassing support in Egypt and Babylon. These regions have been unhappy with Xerxes for some time, and he has had to repeatedly rein the people in. Artaxerxes must be nearing the age of manhood now; he will be ready to fight for the crown soon, if that is where his advisers lead him. I wonder which of the king's advisers has fallen sway to Artaxerxes and his followers, for I know a plan such as this will have a traitor inside the palace as well.

But once again, I am only a spectator to the ruthless plans of men. Once again I must remain silent as the world falls in around me.

48

Thirteenth Day of the Month of Nisan
Twelfth Year of the Reign of Xerxes
Year 3404 after Creation

I did not know I had so many guardians and true friends!

When I awoke this morning, Ashtari had already left the chambers to attend to the court. She had a dispatch of letters to certain nobles on my behalf. One servant begged me for assistance with a younger sister who had poor eyes; the girl needed a job and no one in the village would have her. I wrote a letter to a noblewoman I knew was kindly inclined, telling her this girl would be an excellent servant if hired. Another girl had received word her father had died and her mother was begging at the city gates. I asked a nobleman to take her in; apparently the mother is a marvelous seamstress and both would be thereby blessed.

So I lay in my bed, thinking my day would be slow since all my work had been accomplished through my letters. Within moments, several girls gently prodded me awake, and as I waited for my eyes to clear, they already had me half dressed and into my outer chamber. There stood a man, no taller than me really, with wild hair and a frightened expression. I motioned for him to sit, but he remained standing, so I took the chair instead and waited for someone to tell me what was going on.

He spoke first. "Good queen, I have often carried messages from Mordecai to your servant Stateira. It has been my honor to serve you in this way. I would never have revealed my identity to you, lest you think I sought some reward, but now I must offer it as proof of my allegiance to your crown. Last night news emerged from Xerxes' throne, and I felt compelled to bring you the news immediately, lest time, or your friend, be lost."

I looked from girl to girl, then back to the man. What friend was he referring to?

"As you know," he continued, "the Jews live here in Persia at the mercy and good grace of our king, but they are not truly welcome. They have strange customs and keep to themselves. They have often aroused suspicion and anger that perhaps they are hoarding their monies and treasure for a return journey to their home in Jerusalem, when everyone else is being taxed to finance the dream of Persia that Xerxes has proclaimed. Someone has poisoned the king's mind against these people, and against Mordecai the Jew in particular. Of course, my queen, the king does not know of your friendship with Mordecai, for I have made it my duty to keep your secrets as you wish. But whoever this man is to you, whatever affections you may hold, weigh them carefully now as you decide whether to act."

I began to feel a new fear, a fear that my buried secrets were closer than I had dreamed, and I motioned for him to speak on.

"Because Mordecai will not honor the prime minister, Haman, he has invited his own death. We are helpless indeed to avert that.

But Xerxes will not kill Mordecai alone. Instead, he will order people throughout the province to kill all the Jewish people and seize their wealth. He will spare no one—women, children, the elderly will all fall to the sword on the day he has determined by a toss of the dice. Your friend Mordecai waits outside the palace gates now, in sackcloth and ashes, wailing."

I was stunned. It had been weeks since I had been called to my husband, but how could he have done something so evil? It made no sense from this man of peace. Surely my wild-haired friend was confused on some point. I thanked him and sent him out. Immediately, I ordered Hathach into my chambers. I knew from his expression he had overheard and believed it all to be true.

"Hathach, gather clothes for Mordecai and take them to him at once. Find out what is truly happening, and report back to me immediately."

Hathach left, and I clutched my arms to myself, pacing around the room. My maids, bewildered, tried to pat me on the shoulder and stroke my hair.

"Surely you can save your friend," they crooned to me. "It must be a simple matter of appeasing Haman's pride. Or perhaps you could persuade Mordecai to make a show of paying more taxes to the crown."

Ashtari returned from the outer court. Her face was solemn, and she told the other girls to leave us. Then, alone, Ashtari circled me, silently. She came round to face me, and pointed to the horrible scar on her thigh. "You have seen what a Jew did to me. Why do you weep for this people?" she asked, with cold intention.

She knew.

I was her queen, but in this moment, she ruled.

"Why did you never tell me? Did you fear I could not forgive?" she asked.

"My only fear was that I could never make it up to you," I replied, as softly and honestly as I could. "You have suffered at the hands of a Jew, and there is nothing in my hands that can heal. I would have made your job with me more bitter, and our victory in claiming my crown less sweet. Forgive me now, but keep my secret."

Ashtari's mouth began to tremble. "I was beautiful, until a Jew did this to me. I had a family I loved. I had a chance to be married, to have children! Instead, I was thrown into this palace, never to return to my life! He took everything from me!" She shook me, weeping, and I tried to cradle her in my arms.

"No, Ashtari, not everything. He took your faith, I can see that, but G-d has proved faithful. For you were brought here, to me, and into this palace, where you have been loved and honored all the days I have known you."

She lifted her face to me.

"It is not for us to understand our days," I continued. "We are surrounded by hidden griefs, wounds that we cannot heal. All we can do, in this age, is entrust them to G-d. We don't have answers, but it is not answers we seek. We seek G-d's healing, and I have prayed that for you since the day we met."

Ashtari wept again but wrapped her arms around my neck. "May G-d heal me now!" she cried. "And forgive my hardness of heart! Tell Esther now, G-d, what she is to do in this dark hour!"

Hathach returned shortly with a message from Mordecai. Hathach had a hopeless look about him. He opened his left hand

and a bulletin from the king to the province of Susa fluttered to the floor. It instructed everyone to slaughter the Jews on the thirteenth day of Adar, the twelfth month, and seize their goods and wealth. No one is to be spared on the king's command. Even babies still at the breast must be run clean through.

I felt cold when I read it, and wanted to vomit. This could not have been sealed with the same ring I had worn on my marriage bed! These words did not issue from the mouth that had covered mine in kisses! How had this vile decree come about? My mind could only race and wonder what—or who—had gotten to the king during my absence from him. Did someone in the palace know I was a Jew? Perhaps a harem girl he has grown fond of has put him up to this. Mordecai had refused to bow to Haman—he might expect a lashing, or rebuke—but the entire nation slaughtered? No, there was a reason the Jews were to be exterminated, and as I reflected on Cyrus's words to me in the garden, I began to suspect it was a matter of gold, not pride. I have been tutored well, in this palace, about the darkness of the heart. There is more afoot here than wounded pride.

I must find out more.[1]

---

1 See corresponding commentary on page 285 of the appendix, "Women and Terror: A New Understanding of the War."

49

Thirteenth Day of the Month of Nisan
Twelfth Year of the Reign of Xerxes
Year 3404 after Creation

I called Hagai to my chambers late in the evening and set before him a bowl of figs. He seemed to already know that I would make a request of him, but he trusted me to let the conversation unfold as it must. Finally the moment came to tell him. As I poured our spiced wine into the goblets after we had eaten our fill, I smiled at him and spoke.

"Hagai, you have been a most trusted friend and servant for these years since I was brought here. It was you who delivered me to the king, and now I must ask your help to deliver me from him."

Hagai nodded and sipped his wine slowly. He was the kind of man who would be surprised by nothing, but whether this was his truest character or the result of a lifetime spent in a harem, I do not know.

I went on. "Three things reveal people for who they are: danger, love, and gold. All are at work now in the palace. Hagai, I have a confession." The sadness swept over me, from my own weakness and the dire situation that was at hand. "I let the memory of a boy hold my heart for far too long. And now I long for those nights with the king, before this present wickedness infested our days. Xerxes is a good man, truly, for this evil has made that more clear to me. Wretched woman that I am, for not being able to repay his goodness a thousand times over!"

I covered my face with my hands, and Hagai laid his hands on mine, pulling them away gently, wiping at my tears. G-d had been so good to grant me this third father.

"I have kept many secrets from Xerxes, from you, from this palace, for all of my years here, but they will soon be exposed, for the king has unwittingly signed my death warrant. But there is more here than he knows, for the king's destruction is close at hand," I told him bluntly. The air in the room seemed too heavy, so I rose and opened the curtains to the window on my balcony, letting the night air greet us.

"The desert air here grows only discord and betrayal," I continued, "and I do not know which terror will strike first. The king has made a terrible error at this critical moment, and I am afraid it will set in motion his downfall, and ours. Xerxes has issued a decree to wipe out an entire race of people, the Jews who live in exile here. The king believes it will bring peace and harmony at last, but this act will only line a traitor's pockets with gold for a new war, and fan the passions of the people for a new king. I will be dead, and Xerxes' throne will be ripe for destruction."

Hagai took it all in with a great calmness, his face registering neither fear nor anger. "How may I assist you, my queen?"

"I believe there is one man who holds the key to it all. You must take me to him, tonight."

50

Midnight, Thirteenth Day of the Month of Nisan
Twelfth Year of the Reign of Xerxes
Year 3404 after Creation

"I have dressed many women, but never as this." Hagai smiled. I was drowning in thick, scratchy robes and wondered how I would ever walk the short steps out of my hall down into the courtyards, where I would find the path that led me to the quarters of the Immortals. Only the brooding Magi and the fearsome Immortals were permitted to walk freely among the palaces and grounds. (I had tried to lift the sword Hagai had sneaked into my room, but I stumbled and lost my balance. I could not pass as an Immortal if I could not bear up under their armor, and so a Magi I would be.)

There was a thick breastpiece over the outer robe, with a picture of the sun and moon engraved, and a prayer for Ahura Mazda. He was the god of the sun, but the Persians also believed the moon held special powers for them and they could not bring themselves to swear loyalty to one over the other. That was unfortunate for me, since this made the breastpiece so large I feared my neck wouldn't last the journey. Hagai liked its effect—indeed he thought it was safer to walk as one hobbled by age—and so it worked.

It was strange, so strange, to divest myself of all my jewels, my rings and necklaces and arm bands, and slip unadorned into these robes of idolaters. My feet seemed to be torn open by the rough sandals of leather, when they had been for so long in slippers of silk and fur. How soft I have become from life in the court! Had I once worn robes as plain as this, and even walked barefoot in the hot sands? It is a mercy perhaps that the girls never leave the harem, for I myself have grown too accustomed to comfort. We were flowers of an exotic variety now, and could never survive outside.

Finally, my hair was pinned up and my face hidden by a black hood that cast a long shadow over my features. I looked like a Magi, but tonight I was going to undo a spell, not cast one. Hagai led me carefully out of my chambers and down hallways seldom used, toward the back staircase. No one cast a glance twice as I shuffled past; we were only another set of servants attending the whims of the crown. I had often dreamed of tasting freedom, the way the animals in the fields sometimes chafed at their yokes. I had dreamed of walking down these very stairs and out into the cool of the night. But tonight my mission was freedom of another kind. Perhaps I had held Cyrus's memory in my heart too long, perhaps it set in motion events I could not understand. But I would finish his plan tonight, and save my people.

We walked down the stairs, out into the courtyards, and down another path Hagai seemed to know well. He led me to the edge of the barracks and motioned for me to stop. Taking a few steps forward, he spoke privately with a guard enjoying his evening smoke.

The guard eyed me with disinterest and pointed to a door. Hagai took me by the hand and led me to the door. He leaned in close to whisper, "Once more I lead you to a man's chambers. Once it was for love and glory, and now it is the desperate hope of life. May your G-d bless you in this. I will wait nearby."

The residences here were eerily quiet. Many should have been celebrating the New Year, but few seemed to be awake or even to take notice of my passing. I moved along the passageway of the homes of those who were Immortals. I wondered if they lived like their Spartan equals in Greece, who did not partake in gluttony and drinking. Perhaps the coming execution of the Jews had sobered their minds as they sharpened their swords, and they had not the heart for revelry. All my thoughts were met by the silence around me.

Now I would go into the man I had loved for so long, longer now than the time I had actually known him. I had cried out in my heart for freedom from this place so many times, and I did not know if I had somehow called him to my side, if that was why he committed these acts. What he had spoken of in the garden must never come to be, I see that now. Like our noble forefather Joseph, the sorrows I have borne have turned out to be for my people's deliverance. I can see now that G-d placed me here to save my people, and I will not endanger their lives because my heart was lost to this man so long ago.

Taking a deep breath for courage, I opened the door slowly, finding it unlocked, and stepped inside the room. He was there, polishing his sword and shield, a full goblet sitting close by. He looked up and waved his hand for me to leave.

"I do not have any use for you, my friend." He returned to

polishing, and I could not move. For this was indeed the Cyrus of my dreams, the boy grown into a man, and nothing from my imagination had betrayed me even as I stood only an arm's length away. He was strong and radiated the difficult, wild strength of a man. I realized I had grown too accustomed to being attended to by eunuchs. He was Xerxes' equal in every way, save that this one man had held my heart. I was speechless to view him so plainly. He looked up, and seeing I was still there, reached over the table, grabbed a coin and tossed it at my feet. "Here, if this is what you're after, go and say Cyrus has honored the Magi once more, but leave me now."

I did not remove my hood, but opened my purse concealed in my robes. Gold coins spilled out in a flash of yellow light, covering his floor and making such a noise it startled him as much as the sight.

"I believe it is I who is to bring you gold, Cyrus," I whispered.

He looked from the coins to my face, but he could not see beyond the shadows.

"It is all a matter of coins, is it not?" I asked in a low voice. "You would take the crown not for the people who support it, but for the treasury it guards."

Cyrus jumped to his feet, springing past the table, and shoved me into the door, his arm against my throat. My hood slipped lower over my face but I did not need to see his fury; it was enough to feel it.

"What is this evil you speak of? How is my name involved?" he hissed at me. "I guard the king's life with my own and will let no one muddy my name."

I could not breathe. I found no words to reply but only shook my head.

"You cannot be referring to the king's edict to slaughter the Jewish remnant here," Cyrus said. "I do not have the king's ear, and I do not guide his hand to write." He eased his force against my neck so that I could answer.

"Do you not remember the garden, my love?" I asked, my voice as close to my own as I could allow with his arm crushing me. "If it is only money you want, take this, and go. Leave the Jews in peace and there will be more, much more."

He edged back a bit more, his forehead deeply lined. As he composed himself, he reached for my hood. It slid back easily, and Cyrus mutely stared at me, the queen, his boyhood love, standing in the private chambers of an Immortal.

Finally, he pulled me close and held me. "Who knows you are here?" he whispered.

"Hagai, my palace attendant, has brought me to you, and he is trustworthy." I replied.

"Esther, what is this you have spoken of, and how am I involved?" he asked me again. "You cannot believe I would will the king to destroy our people?"

I began to panic, to feel confused and uncertain. "It is what you told me in the garden. I came here tonight to see if you could be dissuaded. You wanted revenge on Mordecai, on your father, on the Jews who betrayed me to the palace … you wanted me." I did not sound like a woman making statements anymore, only a girl asking stupid questions. I felt afraid, and foolish.

"I have never been in your garden, Esther. Tell me what has happened," he urged me.

I told him, feeling more frightened now because my enemy was unknown, and so perhaps unstoppable. I told him of the gifts, and the clandestine meeting, and his jaw grew set as he listened.

"Esther, you are right, then, that our people and the king are in great danger." He paced for a moment in this sparse room. He barely had length to take three full strides. "The Immortals under my command have been wary of Vashti and Artaxerxes for some time now; we know they are on the move, gaining support and building a war chest. But even so, I do not think this threat springs from them. There must be someone closer to the throne who would topple it."

He turned back to me and touched my cheek for a moment. "You must go back, Esther. You must never return here again." Then, more roughly, he took me by the shoulders and looked in my eyes. "Never risk your life like this again. I have spent a lifetime defending it." He kissed my forehead tenderly, exhaling only once before scooping the money back into my purse and shoving me toward the door.

His voice was a hoarse whisper. "There are Immortals who see the evil in this new decree. We will give the appearance of being ready to carry out his demands, even as we strike down the one who prompted him to write it. The men loyal to me will seek this one and destroy him, my queen. I can promise you this: He will not end your reign, or our people."

Hagai quickly moved to my side, and we made our way back to my palace, and my chambers. I cried silently the whole way. The Magi say the sun illuminates our hearts, but it is here, tonight, in the cool wash of moonlight, that my days have been made plain to me. Once I had been led away from Cyrus to this palace, in trepidation and fear, unwilling to give myself to another. I know now that the memory of Cyrus does not compare to the man, but being everything he is, I can dishonor him no more by wishing he was mine. And now how I long for Xerxes, his goodness disguised by his coarse face and eager touch! I long for what I once had with him, and fear it is no more. Will G-d, will Xerxes, give me another chance?

As we entered my chamber doors, we spied a man in dark clothes slipping over the balcony fleeing my chambers as quickly as he could. Hagai pushed me behind the door and chased after him. But the man was as quick as Yoon-Mai's tiger leaping through the garden. Hagai returned breathless and scoured the chambers, looking for another intruder, be it a man or snake, or other means of quick death. When he turned down the coverings for my bed, a signet ring lay on my pillow with a note: "When the time comes, wear this ring and you will avoid harm from my men." Hagai picked it up and held it close to the torches burning above us. He turned to me to show it; his face had a grim satisfaction.

"This is the mark of the house of Haman," he told me.

51

Fourteenth Day of the Month of Nisan
Twelfth Year of the Reign of Xerxes
Year 3404 after Creation

Hagai posted guards outside my windows, discreetly calling for more servants to attend me for the evening. I was able to bathe and sleep, and record the events of the evening before being interrupted again. Hathach delivered a message from Mordecai, his own plan to quickly end this madness. I could tell Hathach was nervous reading this aloud to me. (No doubt, then, he had read it first.)

> *Greetings from your cousin Mordecai.*
> *You are to go to the king and reveal yourself as a Jew*
> *   at last.*
> *You are to beg Xerxes to spare your people and reverse*
> *   this decree.*

(I rolled my eyes here. Mordecai is so plainly spoken, and naive: In a palace of deception, I was merely to be honest.)

I suspect that the prime minister, Haman, is behind
    the order of slaughter.
Please be on your guard with him until I know more.

Mordecai couldn't know how much more Haman wanted. The blood of the Jews was only to be a lubricant for the wheels of war. A man like Haman sought war never for the thrill of fighting, but only for the greed of plunder. That's a part of what I am to be yet again: plunder.

I could only laugh. It was a death sentence Mordecai gave me. Perhaps I do not know who my enemies in the court are, but I do know the protocol: If I go to the king without first being summoned, I die.[1] No one approaches his throne without an invitation, not even the queen. Especially not the queen, perhaps, given the disrespectful legacy left to me by Vashti. The guards were posted to protect the king's throat, true, but also his honor.

This was Mordecai's grand plan, the sum of his diplomatic skill? I exhaled and clenched my jaw. I mean no disrespect, but I have lived inside the palace for five years, and Mordecai has not spent an hour within these walls.

"I cannot do this," I said to Hathach.

He nodded in agreement, knowing the outcome was a beheading.

"This was no way to save your people," he added. Ashtari tried

---

1 The ancient secular historian Josephus recounts this particular law of Xerxes: "Now the king had made a law, that none of his own people should approach him unless they were called, when he sat upon his throne; and men, with axes in their hands, stood around his throne, in order to punish such as approached to him without being called." *Josephus, The Complete Works,* Translated by William Whiston (Nashville: Thomas Nelson, 1998), 358–359, 11.6.3.

to comfort me, to help me think through this haze of fear, and we finally settled on this message to return to Mordecai:

> *Everyone in the courts, and people throughout the*
> *kingdom, know there is only one fate for the person*
> *who approaches Xerxes' throne uninvited: death.*
> *There is one exception: If the king extends his gold*
> *scepter; then the approaching person may live. No one*
> *has ever dared to test Xerxes' mercy in this manner,*
> *and I am least qualified at the moment, for it's been*
> *thirty days now since I've been invited to come to the*
> *king.*

I found it more difficult to write, with everyone in the chamber watching me, but I finished the letter, and was careful to seal it, catching Hathach's eyes as I pressed my sign into the wax. He blushed and did not miss the point. It is unwise to read another's letters, even if you witnessed them written.

I did add a line no one knew of.

> *Even on the days when my crown is secure, at night*
> *the king's bed never is, and he has found a new*
> *favorite.*

Mordecai had made friends with many servants who moved freely between the palace and the village, yet he could not know what happened behind palace walls all of the time.

I sent Hathach out to deliver our message to Mordecai. If anyone spied Mordecai meeting with Hathach several times in one day, suspicion would be aroused, but with a date set for his execution, I felt he would be indulged. So I asked Hathach to deliver the message and then get to Harbana at once. Harbana has served the king for all of his reign, and must know more of the details I am anxious for.

Hathach left me with great speed. Ashtari went below to fetch me some medicinal tea to soothe my nerves. I should have my answers from both Harbana and Mordecai before nightfall. And now, in the stillness of my chamber—oh, how it once felt like a refuge, and now begins to feel like a tomb!—I have a moment to record these events, and my thoughts. Lord, will You intercede? Have You brought me so far to send me to my death? We were exiled against our will to this land. We kept ourselves separate, to honor You in this land of gods and superstitions. Why has Your wrath been kindled? Must I die and leave the people without an advocate? This can't be Your doing. But are You willing to undo it?

I did what I had been afraid to do since I was brought here six years ago. I moved to the roof and ordered the servants to leave me and wait below. I could not be sure no one was watching me, but I continued. I marked the sun, its position in the sky at this hour, and turned toward the home of my people, the seat of G-d's favor. I turned toward Jerusalem and knelt, then lay down. My hands were outstretched as if I could catch any drop of mercy from heaven, and I, the queen whose beauty had shaken a kingdom, pressed my face into the dust and prayed.

52

Evening, Fourteenth Day of the Month of Nisan
Twelfth Year of the Reign of Xerxes
Year 3404 after Creation

Do not think that because you are in the king's
house you alone of all the Jews will escape. For if you
remain silent at this time, relief and deliverance for
the Jews will arise from another place, but you and
your father's family will perish. And who knows but
that you have come to royal position for such a time
as this?[1]

Hathach repeated the words of Mordecai's message and stood before me, waiting for my reaction. Mordecai's words were less than accommodating. Harbana's message, too, has now left me little room to doubt my course of action: "There is no evidence you have lost the king's favor. The king has not grown enamored of any one girl.

---

1 This message has also been recorded in the sacred texts of both Jews and Christians. Refer to Esther 4:13–14, the *New International Version* of the Bible, or chapter four in the Jewish book of Scripture pertaining to Esther, the Megillah.

Indeed, he has had a different one every night in your absence."
Hathach shook his head at the message, and I almost smiled. Some
people have a gift for wounding you with their comforting words.
Ashtari watched me carefully as I received the messages; I wondered
what she felt. She had never been allowed to share her bed; I had
been forced to share mine with many rivals. There were times in my
distress I caught her looking strangely at me, and I wondered if it
was pity or envy.

My time on the roof had yielded no certain words. I was frightened to have sought G-d so earnestly and received nothing for my
hour of need. If G-d had denied me an audience, what did this mean
for the hour when I would seek the same from Xerxes?

A bird flew in my window, resting on the ledge and singing
sweetly. For a moment we were all transfixed by the visitor, and
she bobbed her head and looked at us with a pleasant eye. In the
silence that enveloped us, I heard in my mind a verse from Solomon:
*Through patience a ruler can be persuaded, and a gentle tongue can
break a bone.* The bird sang again, and I marveled at its fragile wings,
wings that were yet able to beat back the winds and carry it wherever
it desired to go.

"That is my answer!" I said aloud.

Everyone turned to look at me, their expressions betraying their
confusion.

"I am a weak creation," I said. "I sought great strength from G-d
to meet this evil. But my weakness is to be my strength. Deliver this
final message to Mordecai for me tonight," I instructed Hathach.
"Tell Mordecai: Gather all the elders of the Jewish people, and send
this message throughout Susa to all Jews: You must fast for me. Don't

eat or drink for three days, either day or night. I, and my servants, will fast as well.[2] Do not pledge to me your strength or money. Give to me your weakness. If you will lift me up to G-d through your prayers and suffering, I'll go to the king, even though it's forbidden. If I die, I die."

As Hathach turned to leave, I grabbed his hand and held it as I spoke. Hathach had the soft, smooth skin of a court eunuch, but I sensed he loved loyalty above comfort. He knew my secret now too, but I was not afraid. "You have been a faithful friend, Hathach. Sleep in peace when you return tonight. May G-d smile on you for helping my people."

"And may your G-d smile on this plan," Hathach replied as he turned to leave.

I do not know what will happen now, what G-d intends with this new plan. I have laughed at the seers who read the future in tea leaves, but I have often been no different, trying to divine G-d's will in events. I watched Hathach leave and wrapped my arms around myself as if I were cold.

I wonder if I will live to see him again.

---

2 Fasting, a Jewish custom still practiced today, involved refusing food and drink for a predetermined period of time in order to devote oneself to prayer and meditation. The Jews believed that lessening the distractions of the physical world enabled one to better discern God's will and receive God's blessing.

53

Sixteenth Day of the Month of Nisan
Twelfth Year of the Reign of Xerxes
Year 3404 after Creation

The days of fasting gave me no real answers and no sudden reassurances. In a land where women are stripped of all power, I have been chosen to confront a most powerful enemy. My mind turned the words from Solomon over and over, and I meditated on the ways of patience and gentleness. I am reminded of what Mordecai taught me as a girl: It is one thing to believe a Scripture is true; it is another thing entirely to trust in it and act.

The robe I wore for my coronation still drapes as lovely as it did that evening so many years ago. Has it really been five years since I first came to Xerxes? Once again, the girls have prepared me as rigorously as that first night with the king, when I first laid eyes on the man who would be my king, my lover, my captor, and my shield. My jewels rest over my body like a waterfall from heaven. The largest ruby, set in gold and surrounded by turquoise, is nestled between my breasts, just barely revealed in my dress beneath the mantle of gold and rubies. The harem girls are famous for baring all at once; I am playing a slower and more serious game: calling him to remember, and imagine. To draw him in so that we may both be revealed.

There are no roses tonight for my hair. I came to this palace an exile, and if I must die, I will die exiled even from those. The girls circled me slowly as they combed the last strand of hair, and smoothed the last fold of dress. We are all weak from hunger and despair. Only Ashtari has served to keep our minds on our work. She has been relentless, explaining to the other girls the perilous mission (it was not lost on them that if I fail, they will be lost when a new queen comes into power). Ashtari has sent word to the kitchen staff to prepare a feast for lovers, with foods to be eaten slowly, served with grace. I must have every opportunity, should I live, to serve the king and honor him in front of our guest. It is true that I am sick with hunger. If left alone, I could probably devour everything put in front of me. But I must serve the king first as if my only appetite is for him. Perhaps I will not be able to eat in the presence of Haman. King David once promised that G-d will teach us to feast in the presence of our enemies, and I must believe that too.

And so it is time to go.

I will be led, once again, and perhaps for the last time, to the man who can behead me, or take me to his bed, according to his mood. You have made me queen, Lord, and given me riches beyond my dreams. Is it too much to ask now for my life? And if You give me my life, will You give me the nation of Jews as well?[1]

---

1 Josephus's writings confirm Esther's account here but add the detail that Esther, weak from hunger, required two handmaidens to support her and the weight of her robes and train as she made her approach to the king.

54

Evening, Sixteenth Day of the Month of Nisan
Twelfth Year of the Reign of Xerxes
Year 3404 after Creation

I stood in the inner court of the palace, where I had been led past servants and advisers conferring over the kingdom's affairs; they were all now startled to see me in my royal robes approaching the king unannounced. A few of the more decent ones managed to recover in time to bow their heads in respect as I passed. The king must have been conducting official business, because all of his advisers were present, and I could hear more muted voices from inside the king's throne room as I approached. I reached the center of the outer court, stood, and waited. What would Xerxes see when he looked up? Would he see the woman he loved, or the bride who had betrayed him, if only in her heart?

I could see Xerxes on his throne, surrounded by several men pushing scrolls toward him, and a eunuch who was fanning him in the late-day heat. Xerxes caught sight of my robe, first, I think, as the jewels reflected the afternoon light into a thousand red arcs across the mosaic floor. He stopped a moment to take in my vision, and I held my breath.

Smiling broadly, his eyes held me there a moment, and all eyes turned to me. I had risked death to offer myself to him. My plain desire, my need of him, was not lost on his vanity. The men in the throne room immediately bowed and backed out of the room, and his smile grew wider. His eunuch, Harbana, handed him the golden scepter, and Xerxes extended it to me now.

I walked boldly, my chin quivering and eyes blinking back the hot tears of relief, and touched the tip of the scepter.

"What is your heart's desire, my beloved queen? What do you want from your king? Just ask me now and it will be yours—even if it's half my kingdom!" He said this so loudly I knew all standing outside had heard.

His eyes were undressing me even now and I could not help but force back a laugh. Thirty days' absence had served me well. It gave me courage that he was eager to see me, and ready to give me so much.

"My good king knows I have never asked for gold or kingdoms. But if it should please my king," I replied, bowing again low to the ground so everyone would see the esteem I held him in, "let my king come, with Haman, to a dinner I've prepared for him. Give me what is rightfully mine as your queen: an evening to honor and serve you."

Xerxes' eyes brightened immediately—a feast would be a welcome distraction from the tedious affairs of running a kingdom.

"Get Haman at once," Xerxes commanded Harbana, "and we will go to dinner with Queen Esther."

I bowed before the king once more and kissed his hand as he returned me to my feet. "The king has honored me above all women, all the days I have known you. You will recline on my bosom tonight, and remember why you made me queen."

With that, I exited carefully backward, taking care to show everyone in the palace and inner court that I honored the king in every way. I was led by another palace eunuch to the banquet hall that Ashtari had commanded to be prepared. It was, truly, perfect. Candles and flowers, cascading green vines surrounded a gold, carved table laden heavy with baskets of cherries and walnuts, bowls of honey and oil, roasted lamb with leeks and onions and the sultry scent of saffron drifting from a stew of meat. Bread, nearly white from the care taken in grinding the wheat, had split open from the oven heat, and its hot breath was escaping into the room. A pitcher of cream nestled next to a platter of berries.

I was still taking it in, and silently praising Ashtari for her excellence, when the king was announced. I turned and bowed low, and when I rose I saw that he was followed in by Haman. Up close I understood the continual gossip that he was the most handsome man the courts had ever hosted. He did not walk; he strode into the room, as if every step claimed his own rightful territory. Seeing Haman made me wonder for a moment if G-d took greater care in crafting some of us, for truly this man was perfect. Yet something rotten leeched from his skin and hung from his teeth when he smiled at me. I steeled my shoulders as he took me in. And he did, his eyes moving carelessly over me, too familiar in the king's presence. I could not have anticipated this. For an instant I hoped Xerxes would seize upon the man and I could be done with him, but Xerxes paid no notice. He was already sampling the temptations laid before him.

I stretched a thin smile at Haman and gestured to him to sit. He reclined against a yellow silk cushion and spread a lamb's fleece under his feet. The king chose his favorite—a purple cushion that the Egyptian servants have described as bearing a resemblance to a hippopotamus. But it enveloped him and it took no minor adjustment to position myself behind him, so that he could recline against my bosom to be fed. The evening was only beginning, but as I poured the wine for the king (I let Haman be served by the table eunuchs), he was high in spirits.

"Now, what is it you want, my beloved? I would give you half of all I own, if you would but ask!" Xerxes implored. One hand was running down the length of my dress, the other was clutching his goblet.

Haman's eyes had not left mine, or my body, since he first entered. He followed Xerxes' hand as it traveled, over the dress, down my thigh. He paid notice to the jewel tucked into my bosom and when he licked his lips after a sip of wine, I wondered what taste was in his mouth. I noted that his dagger was at his side, which was not the custom of the men of the court.

But it was not yet time.

"Here's what I want," I replied to Xerxes and ran my fingers through his hair gently. Haman's eyes followed my every move, and both men stopped drinking their wine to listen for my request. What crisis had prompted his queen to ask for an audience? What would he give up tonight? Another jewel? Some prize from the treasury?

"If the king favors me and is pleased to do what I desire and ask," I paused, "let the king and Haman come again tomorrow to the dinner that I will fix for them."

Haman smiled at me, and took another deep draught of wine as his gaze lingered like the wet lick of a dog on my face. I could not know what Haman was imagining as the reason for my repeated invitation. In his wretched imagination and vain ambition, all was possible. His was the voice I had heard that night, the serpent in the garden. Perhaps he thought that his words had prompted my own impatience to end Xerxes' reign and at last be in another's arms.

Xerxes exhaled and laughed, and raised his glass in a toast. He plainly understood me to mean I wanted nothing but his company. Perhaps tomorrow night I would merely chide him for having not called me for these thirty days. He raised his cup and toasted Haman and me: "Let us feast tonight, and return tomorrow for more pleasures."

We did. I made a careful point to exit the feast as the last of the wine was being opened.

"Drink a cup for loyalty to the crown," I proposed as I made my way to the door. I hoped my words were not lost on Haman. They were certainly lost on Xerxes, who, although having eaten everything I put before him, looked as if I had only awakened his appetite. He was not entirely pleased to see me go.

The girls were waiting up for me, all perched on the edges of the chairs and the bed in my chambers. They leaped to their feet when they saw me, searching my face for some clue of the outcome.

"I said nothing. Tomorrow night we will feast again."

A few girls just stared, and a few groaned. Only one spoke up: "Will we fast, then, until tomorrow night?"

I was so weary, from the fast of three days, from the fever-pitch of fear, that I could only smile at her question and shake my head no. "If you have not eaten yet, please send to the kitchen for a sample of the banquet to be brought to your room at my command. It is time to eat, and let our fate rest on shoulders other than our own. The events have been set in motion, and G-d is aware of our plan." I patted the servant girl on her hand.

Finally Ashtari spoke. I sensed her confusion, and wondered if it was fear or anger making her want the conclusion tonight, and not tomorrow.

"Why, Queen Esther, why did you not speak tonight?" she asked.

I met her eyes. "Ashtari, when you grab a serpent by the neck, if you let go too soon, will it not bite you? I must be sure Haman's fate is sealed, his neck broken, before I release him back to the king."

The answer hung in the air, and the girls turned slowly to return to their bedchambers for the night. Only Ashtari remained and helped me prepare for bed. Her hands were steady and gentle as she brushed out my hair. Although we spoke little, I knew she was not at peace with my decision to prolong our agony.

Later that night, I slept fitfully. The wine and rich foods burned in my stomach. Three days of fasting had prepared my spirit but had done little for my body. The evening weighed heavily in my dreams, too, and Haman appeared to me over and over, standing over my bed, his hands finding me in the darkness, his smile dripping a poison that burned my eyes. With each rotted nightmare I jolted awake, but Ashtari was there, wiping my brow and smoothing the silk coverlet back down. My eyes were only stinging from tears and exhaustion, she explained; Haman had not been in the room.

Somewhere in the palace another set of workers was preparing the next feast, and still more were riding out into the countryside in search of more delicacies and delights to adorn the table. When at last I could sleep no more, I rose and looked out my balcony. It seemed to me the sun had not slept well, either. It was making a mean entrance in the horizon.

My thoughts turned to Mordecai, and what he was doing. He must know by now that I am still at least alive, although the Jews' fate was still undecided. But what of him? Will Haman touch him before the day of the slaughter? Is Mordecai yet alive?

55

Hathach wasted no time appearing in my chambers this morning. The maids were still urging me to drink some warm tea to soothe my stomach and my worried brow when he arrived with news about Mordecai.

"A message from Mordecai?" I asked eagerly.

"No," he replied. "I have not spoken to Mordecai. I have brought news about Mordecai, however, and something of interest transpiring in the king's palace."

I urged him on.

"Haman intends to kill Mordecai today, before the feast tonight," he said.

I cried out and a maid ran forward to steady me.

"Something had spurred him to put his plan in motion at once rather than wait," Hathach said. "Haman has ordered a gallows built, seventy-five feet high. He has planned to hang Mordecai on it, publicly, after he has arranged it with the king. In fact, Haman went

227

to the king this morning, before dawn, to have Mordecai's death warrant sealed."

My head was in my hands and I could not steady myself even to look up.

"But, good queen," he quickly added, seeing my distress, "Harbana brought me news of Mordecai that may yet delay his fate. I do fear, though, the cure is worse than the disease, for it may provoke Haman to a rash act that would certainly be Mordecai's final undoing," Hathach said, his voice trailing away as if in thought.

I looked up at him, and he continued.

"My queen, Harbana told me the king could not find sleep last night. As is his custom, he ordered his records be brought in and read to him. As chance would have it, or perhaps as your G-d would have it, out of Xerxes' twelve-year reign, the passage that the records keepers turned first to was a story about Mordecai's loyalty to the crown in exposing the murderous plot of Bigthana and Teresh. Even while Haman was waiting in the outside chamber to ask for Mordecai's head, the king was being reminded of Mordecai's faithful service. Who else but your G-d could have planned that?" he asked me in awe before continuing recounting the drama to me:

"The king was startled to remember this account, and he sat up in his bed. 'What great honor was given to Mordecai for this?' the king asked. 'Nothing,' the records keeper and attendants replied. 'Nothing has been done for him!' the servant added again for emphasis. It had not been hard for them to remember a faithful servant to the crown who had been slighted. The king, seized with an idea, stood up and asked if anyone was in the outer court. There were no advisers at that hour, except for Haman, who had just arrived from building the gallows.

"The king ordered him brought in, and posed this question: 'Tell me, Haman, what honor would be most fitting for the man who has served the king well, and deserves recognition?'

"Surely Haman had nursed just such a question for years, because Harbana says his answer was swift and sure: 'Long live the king for his generous hand to his faithful servants! This man would be most honored, my king, to wear a robe that the king has worn in ceremony,[1] and to ride a horse the king has ridden in a royal procession. This man's good name would be secured for all generations if the king would have a nobleman lead him on horseback through the city, calling out to the people, "This man is highly favored and honored above all men by the king!"'

"So it is being done," Hathach finished. "Mordecai is riding through the streets, led by Haman, and probably right past the gallows Haman has built." Hathach paused to laugh, shaking his head as if he was shaking away the tension.

The servants broke into giggles as well—rumors of Haman had rippled throughout the court for months now. He was not known for his patience with their own mistakes when serving him or his honorable treatment of the youngest servant girls.

But then Hathach grew serious again: "Mordecai is alive, for the moment, but Haman's wrath is sorely provoked now. I do not know what will happen; Haman will not risk a public murder so soon after

---

1 Haman is not simply asking for a piece of clothing, but in fact, a fortune: The robes the king wore in ceremony and receiving visitors from his throne were woven out of gold, with rows of precious stones between the stitches. Haman is asking here for riches and honor allowed only a king.

this great honor, but in the common streets, who is to say a stranger cannot be persuaded to finish the work?"

Hathach looked at me intently before he left as Ashtari put her hand on my shoulder. "May you find success tonight, my queen," he offered.[2]

2 See corresponding commentary on page 286 of the appendix.

56

I was led down the corridor through the king's palace once more. I had chosen this time to wear a royal robe of white fabric, with settings of turquoise beaded into the blue sash I wore at my waist. Golden ropes hung from my hands and ankles, and my hair had only been swept back loosely; strands hung down to frame my face and neck, and the king could undo the pearl pick holding it in place with one hand, if he wished. The girls had painted my eyes with ground malachite, setting them off with a brush of green on top, and a deep black line beneath. My lips were a deep red, and I wondered if my face was flush to match. Deep in the bosom of my robe I had tucked a lotus flower, so that its scent would rise to Xerxes as he kissed me. With that final touch, I had done whatever I could think of to make myself inviting. I knew the banquet would be inviting as well.

I was confident of my cause, and my preparation, but not of my king. From Hathach's report, I knew Haman had not revealed himself entirely to the king. Xerxes did not even know Mordecai was a Jew, and thus one selected for slaughter by Haman. I wondered if the king even understood what he had signed when he handed the Jews over for destruction. Xerxes was famous for the number of massive projects he undertook: extensive highway systems, unheard of before his time; seats of government throughout his kingdom; civil laws and procedures, tax codes and systems that were complex. It was no secret that he signed so many royal decrees he barely had time or inclination to read them carefully. He was a man given to action, not details. His enemy had found his one true flaw and aimed neatly.

When I revealed the truth, when I was at last unveiled as a Jew doomed before him, and his rash decision was exposed for the foolishness that it was, how would he react? Would he be angrier that he had been tricked so easily, or that he had been betrayed by his closest adviser? I thought of the cobra charmers that entertain the court. They knew how to focus the snake and thus control his venom if he struck. I had done well to survive in the courts this long, but when Xerxes' anger was aroused, who would be safe? Xerxes had been betrayed once by a woman he loved and would not suffer it again. Wounds of the heart that have not healed often control what our hands find to do. Could he be trusted to see clearly who had betrayed him? Would he understand that I must save my people and defy the crown as the surest course to safeguarding the honor of his reign?

As I approached the banquet hall, a very young eunuch ran forward and pressed a note in my hands before fleeing back down the hall.

Beware.

Haman has not acted alone.

But neither will you face this night alone, for I have commanded the Immortals to guard the banquet hall with triple their normal numbers. If you are in danger, from Haman or the king, scream and my men will break into the hall and carry you to safety. If this happens, you are to meet me on our mountain, where together we will decide if you will return to the palace. Once again, we will entrust our fate to others.

Cyrus

It was a grace to know Cyrus was ready to save my life, and a torment to think of new endings to this story that would never be. I would save my people tonight, or die in the palace that took me from them.

The doors to the banquet hall opened, and I was pleased. The table had been set much as before, but now copper mirrors reflected the light from the candles all around, and fresh red roses were a scarlet river running down the center of the table. Tears came to my eyes as I took in their scent. I had once been a girl who prayed the scent of these roses would return to her with a hint of adventure; now I longed for them to bring me a remembrance of home, and of quiet, simple days.

The doors opened behind me and I turned to face my guests. Haman entered first. He was richly dressed but looked disheveled somehow; I could not put my finger on what was out of place. Perhaps it was only his heart, or conscience, if such a man can have one, that was unkempt and ill at ease. There was something new in his eyes tonight, something I have not often seen so raw in this palace. Fear. It almost overshadowed the sultry cravings I could see were still alive.

Then the king was announced and made his entrance. I smiled, a smile free and honest when I saw how innocent he was of the treachery he was walking into. I felt sorry that I had never been able to reveal my secret to him. I would be glad to tell him everything at last. If I lived. To survive this night, I had to direct his venom toward Haman.

I felt unsteady as I led Xerxes to his seat. Women in his kingdom were but dressing for a man's bed and a satisfactory way to provide heirs. The king had once banished a queen on the advice of his counsel. Now would he accept the word of his queen and banish the adviser? *Dear G-d*, I pleaded silently, *how can it be that I should change history? I am a prisoner myself—how can I ask for the freedom of a nation?*

The eunuchs began pouring the wine, and the king settled comfortably against me. He did not seem to notice that his companions were in private distress. I took a long, deep drink of the wine and let my fingers run through his hair, as I might have done on any occasion. I noticed Haman gripping his cup tightly, his mind somewhere else. Eunuchs hovered over him, refilling the wine much faster and more frequently than I had seen the previous night. The soft music of the lyre filled the room, and as I traced my fingers down along the side of the king's face, I could tell he was closing his eyes, enjoying the moment. Nearly all his senses were sated now, and for Xerxes, this was a good night. In between sips of his wine, I fed him pistachios.

The three of us found little to speak of, but Xerxes took this in as if we, too, had been transported by the evening.

When they began clearing the center table for the main dish, Xerxes propped himself up on one elbow and turned himself a bit to look at me.

"Queen Esther," he asked, "what is it you want, my beloved? I would give you half of all I own, if you would but ask!" He loved being so generous in front of Haman, showing he could give away half a kingdom and not miss it. Had he but known I would ask for so much more. His steady stare told me he expected a reply tonight, in earnest. It seemed no one moved as I fought for the words to come next.

My courage escaped me suddenly, and I wet my lips as I paused. I met Xerxes' eyes, and my mind seemed to fall back suddenly, through a thousand nights, to the first evening I had been brought to his chambers. I remembered his first caress, and the look in his eyes when he had slipped his ring on my finger. I remembered how he slowly drew me into his dreams, dreams of a kingdom ruled by justice and order. He would lose his dream, by his own hand, if I did not act and act well.

"I was brought to you with nothing, good king," I said. "You have given me all I have. You have given me yourself, a gift I was not worthy of. Yet I am forced now to ask for more. Forgive me. I must ask my king for two things tonight: my life, and the lives of my people. My people have been betrayed, our necks brought low under your mighty sword. You, too, my beloved, have been betrayed because you were not told who it was you were to destroy. You would kill me, your queen, and all of my people by a decree issued from this court in recent days."

Xerxes exploded, "I would never do such a thing! Your foolish maids have lied to you, as I swear by my throne, Esther!"

I shook my head, not meeting his eyes. "No, my Lord, I have seen the decree signed by your own ring. You ordered the massacre of my people, and by your decree I must die too. For I have held a secret from you all these years. When I was a girl, I was a simple thing who tended roses and lambs, and was orphaned too young. That is what you know of my past, and that much is true. But there is always more to a tale than is told at first passing, and what I kept from you I will tell now. For I was raised by Mordecai, the Jew who often is at the king's gates conducting minor business for the court, while I tended our stall in the market. I, too, am a Jew. It is true that your father who sat before you on the throne was good and kind to the Jews, and I have nothing to fear from you. But there is among us a people who were once bent on destroying the Jews, every last one of us, down to the mothers and the babies in their wombs. Many generations ago, G-d granted my people one battle, a battle to wipe this menace from this land forever, and completely. But our hand faltered when we wielded the sword of G-d. We committed a great sin by allowing our enemy to live on. We were unable to do what must be done. We believed too much in the hope of change in men's hearts. We believed that the past was a dead and silent thing. I am sorry that the mistake of our past now reaches out to strip you of your good name. I must ask you tonight to reverse your order. No king has ever reversed a royal decree, this I know, but I beg you not to stand on the tradition of dead men who only crumble away beneath you. Reverse the decree and punish the man who presented it to you."

"Who is it, Esther? Who is the traitor? He will pay with more than his life!" Xerxes commanded.

"The traitor is the one who has shared your bread, and your wine, and would share your queen if his plan to overthrow your crown would succeed. The traitor's plan would perhaps have been perfect, save he did not know that I am a Jew as well. I wonder, Haman, as you are a man of many details and plans, how this fact eluded you?" I said, turning now to face the dog himself.

Xerxes wrenched himself to his feet, glowering at Haman, who was still reclining on his cushions, searching for his voice. Haman almost replied, but only little gulps of air went in his mouth, and he could not expel any words with them and instead waved his arms a bit. Finding he had no words that would placate the king, Haman then filled with rage. Haman's powerful arm swept his place setting cleanly to the floor, and he brought a fist down on my elegant table. His eyes unveiled the bitter bloodlust of his dreams, and he glared at Xerxes. Haman rose from his cushions and stood, the two men staring at each other across the large table. The eunuchs standing at their posts all along the walls glanced around the room in panic, unsure if the guards outside the door had heard, and would now arrest Haman immediately. Everyone waited for Xerxes' command.

But Xerxes stormed out. As he threw back the doors, I heard a tremendous violence. Apparently the main course had arrived, and Xerxes had sent it sprawling down the corridor when the doors smashed into the platters. Confused servants scattered about, unsure how to serve us during this calamity. Haman found his words now and his tone was much softer than the hate burning in his eyes moments earlier.

"Good Queen Esther, save me from this error," he said. "The Jews have been speaking in such harsh ways about you. They are jealous, I can see that now, the way lesser sisters envy the prettiest. I sought only to be free of them, and to have you, because your great beauty compels me. Forgive me as you would forgive any of love's fools. You cannot know the pain of loving one you cannot hold." He tore his robe and ran his hands over his face in anguish.

I turned my face from his pleas, and he came around the table to crouch near me. He had torn his robe so that his chest was plainly seen, the great muscles no longer straining at the fabric covering them.

"I know what you feel for Xerxes. I know that you do not love him," he said, his voice low. "I can give you what he cannot." Haman cast a pointed glance out the balcony. "I can give you your freedom."

I would not look directly at him. He moved closer to take my hands in his, and I protested loudly. Instinctively, his hand went over my mouth as his eyes swept the room. I struggled to get free and Haman lost his balance, lurching onto me. His hand now dislodged from my mouth, I screamed.

The doors flew open, their heavy cedar wood nearly shattering from the force, as Xerxes and a storm of Immortals broke in at the same time. The Immortals ran for me, leaping over the table, wrenching Haman off of me by his neck. One Immortal grabbed me, and I felt him begin to lift me over his shoulder to rescue me at Cyrus's command. "Let me down! It is Haman who is in danger, not me!" I hissed to him, and he released me.

Xerxes roared, "Dare Haman rape the queen while I'm deciding his fate?"

Haman froze, terror gripping him tightly. He wasn't even aware that he was still clutching a gold chain he had torn from my robe.

Harbana, the king's eunuch, spoke first. "Look over there!" He pointed to the view just beyond the windows of the hall. "Those gallows were built by Haman to hang Mordecai publicly, the servant who saved the king's life!"

The king moved his stare from Harbana to Haman, and then to the guards. Xerxes' voice grew cold and stinging. "You are indeed a man of details, Haman, and I thank you for the foresight. Harbana, call Cyrus, the Chief of the Immortals, and have him hang Haman on the gallows,"[1] he commanded.

The guards picked up the stricken Haman and led him away. Xerxes commanded that we be left alone. He came to me as I reclined and took my hands in his tenderly.

"What have I done, my queen?" he asked. The weight of the years, of the kept secrets and shaded heart came tumbling down now as I revealed my truest love for him. I pressed the back of his hand against my cheek and let my tears fall at last. He called out for a guard to enter.

"Find this man Mordecai and bring him to us immediately," Xerxes commanded. I hoped it was to be Mordecai who would enter next, and not a messenger telling us we had acted too late. Xerxes held me while we waited.

When Mordecai arrived, I threw my arms around him and wept again. To be reunited at last with my cousin, my only family, was

---

1 Hanging did not mean the form of punishment Western civilization has come to know. Rather, hanging involved impaling a man on an enormous pole and allowing him to hang this way until death.

sweeter than I had imagined it. Mordecai had aged much in these years apart. He was no longer a simple man, concerned with the affairs of a market and tending to his duties at the king's gates. He, too, had carried the weight of the crown for too long. Together, we turned now to face Xerxes, and I fell at Xerxes' feet. He extended his golden scepter to me, and I knew I could stand.

"If it would please my beloved king, if I am indeed in your good graces, please let an order be written to reverse Haman's evil decree to slaughter the Jews. I am your queen, and loyal forever to your throne, but how could I live content if I saw my people's blood running in the streets? You are always eager to give me half of your kingdom, but I would not ask so much. I merely ask for this remnant of people."

Xerxes said the one thing I had not expected him to say, if my plan had carried this far.

He said no.

"My Star," he said sadly, "no king of Persia has ever reversed himself, for it cannot be done. My word will stand."

What could I do, but nod in mute accord? I had asked and been refused.

Xerxes looked at us and smiled softly. "I will do this one thing, however: Together with Mordecai, write whatever you decide on behalf of the Jews; then bring it to me and I will seal it with my signet ring. Perhaps you will find a way to do better for your people than reversing the decree. And Haman's estate will belong now to you, Queen Esther. Dispose of it as you will, even as he's being hanged on the gallows. No enemy of yours will stand while I have the strength to wear my crown."

Mordecai requested he be given time to pray before we wrote a new decree of our own. This pleased the king, who ordered him to be escorted to a fine room in the palace for as long as he wished. Mordecai left, and I was again alone with my king. He turned to me, walking slowly as he studied me. "Tell me, Esther my Star," he said, "you have lived secretly as a Jew with a king who worshipped another god. Tell me what other secrets you have kept from me."

"My king, there is nothing more to reveal," I replied.

I could tell he didn't believe me, but he smiled now. "There is always more to be revealed, my love." His mouth turned up at one end, and his hands moved to the small of my back.

57

*Twenty-third Day of the Month of Sivan
Twelfth Year of the Reign of Xerxes
Year 3404 after Creation*

How quickly Mordecai has established himself within the king's palace! He at once removed men who were under suspicion, including both servants and advisers. The eunuchs who care for me have proved an excellent source of uncovering intrigue. How loose their lips are, it seems, when they are at their chores and out of my sight! Mordecai has taken great pains to protect the king, and not further himself, so that Mordecai is a most-trusted adviser, having replaced Haman's wicked counsel with earnest wisdom. The king brought his secretaries into the court today when he was on his throne and both Mordecai and I were in his presence. Mordecai had counseled me as to what we should propose to the king, and I instructed Mordecai on what would most please the king. The secretaries recorded my words as Mordecai dictated our new decree for the original day of slaughter set by Haman:

*To all satraps, governors, and officials of
the provinces from India to Ethiopia*

a proclamation from the Great King Xerxes:
signed with his ring on this date,
the twelfth year of his reign.
No enemy of the Jews will stand.
Every Jew in every province should be ready,
armed and prepared with the king's good blessing,
to kill anyone who threatens their family.
The Jews alone may decide who their
enemies are, and who they must kill.
And if an enemy of the Jews is killed, this
enemy's estate will become the rightful
property of the avenging Jew.
This order goes into effect on the thirteenth day
of the twelfth month, the month of Adar.

When Mordecai had finished dictating this decree, the king summoned his scribes, who worked quickly to transcribe it into the native languages of the kingdom. Xerxes then summoned a hundred couriers, commanding them to ride the fastest horses from his stables, and ordered them to take these notices to every province in the kingdom. They were to be posted publicly for the Jews and their enemies to read and understand. A notice was promptly posted in the capital city of Susa, where the palace resided, as well. By nightfall the Jews would learn their deliverance was secure, and Haman's accomplices would see clearly their doom approaching.

Mordecai will then be a hero among his people, and their hearts will be merry and light when they learn their queen is a Jew as well.

Xerxes then called Mordecai forward and waved the palace

eunuchs toward him. The eunuchs began to dress Mordecai in a purple and white robe, with a gold crown and cape of softest linen.

"May a thousand years of peace reign in my kingdom because of your great wisdom. May your people live in ease, knowing you will always stand before my throne" was the king's blessing.

Mordecai bowed low and lifted his hands, saying, "I give glory to G-d, who has been at work in this palace, and in our lives, long before we were aware of His movements. And I credit my fair cousin for her strength, the strength of ten thousand Immortals, to persevere and win the crown, your heart, and her people."

58

First Day of the Month of Adar
Thirteenth Year of the Reign of Xerxes
Year 3405 after Creation

In just twelve days, the king's orders will come into effect. Hathach has brought me reports from the city, and Mordecai, who comes and goes freely from the palace into the city and back, has confirmed his word. The Jews, once exiles here who only sought quiet refuge and to be left alone, are wild with delight at the thought of war upon their enemies. They have been given a second chance, and they have been held under thumb for too long. The women in particular are ready for bloodshed. They have had many nights of nightmares now, having seen their children's death warrants signed and posted, while wine flows freely in the houses where Haman's men have been sharpening their blades. Now revenge is unleashed, even before the evil can be struck. And there is no vengeance as swift and terrible as a mother's when she has seen her children held over the grave.

Yet I long to see pure righteousness restored in the land. Neighbor is now turned against neighbor; passions so enflamed do not burn down so easily. Mordecai tells me that whispers now take the place of laughter in the market square. When the day comes for my people to attack the enemy, will we seek a final justice and peace, or a mad revenge that leads to more war? My people are on the brink of their divine moment, but will they lose their way? I fear for the vision of Persia that Xerxes holds dear. He had not foreseen a race war in his land. Wars have always been between kingdoms and crowns; now it is an irrational, ancient hatred of the Jews that forces the crisis. My people hold so much more in their hands than their own fates. For civil war could be unleashed here, and what Jew wants to die in exile from Jerusalem? Have they forgotten our call to return and rebuild?

Nothing can bring back the lost years. We had been exiled by war, and by our own rebellious hand against G-d, from our Holy Land. This war in the provinces was not going to restore that blessing again. I began to wonder what the Jews would be fighting for, in their hearts.

I fasted and prayed once more, as I considered the destiny before my people. Yes, a great victory might be obtained. But will they draw close to G-d now, return and be comforted, or will they reopen their wounds by their own swords, rush out without G-d into their day of destiny? Do they still feel their need for G-d now that deliverance is theirs?

Why, I asked Xerxes, why could he not reverse the decree? Why does he force us to meet the moment? It is true that the king's word is law, a law that cannot be altered. Was it pride that kept him from breaking this tradition? But when I asked, Xerxes gave me a reason I had not anticipated, a wise reason that gave me pause.

"If you loose a bag of feathers on a hill, how many can you retrieve, my Star?" he asked.

"None, my lord," I replied.

"And so it is with the evil in men's hearts. Haman's law loosed a vile ambition that I could never have recalled. Your enemies have risen up, and you must kill them." There was a sorrow in his words that moved me. He was not eager to see blood spilled in his land, to see a people governed peaceably turn against each other. "You must pray to your G-d that the Jews will find lasting peace with the peoples of this land."

59

*Thirteenth Day of the Month of Adar
Thirteenth Year of the Reign of Xerxes
Year 3405 after Creation*

Jews have gathered in every city in every province, to make war upon anyone who raises a sword against a Jew. Any known enemy of the Jews knows they will die today. Mordecai has been so honored by the king that people understand Xerxes to be well on the side of the Jews. I imagine by now they have heard that I am a Jew as well. I have heard reports that many people have converted just to escape the sword. Even Cyrus's father, once so eager to assimilate unnoticed into the culture, makes a show now of his Jewish heritage. He greets the rabbis loudly in the marketplace, when once he would have hurried by and pretended not to know them. Cyrus has sent me this report. He confirms that my enemies are well-known to him and will meet his sword today. Cyrus's letter also contained these words, which I wish he had either omitted or named the men more directly:

> *The men who helped Haman seek the throne have
> fled. It is believed they left under the cover of night,*

as dawn approached our city. They were dressed as women, long veils of black covering their heads and faces. But it is not the custom in Susa to wear the robes down to the floor, and I wonder why the guards did not notice hairy ankles slipping by! Perhaps the darkness was indeed a perfect escort. I fear these men, my queen, I fear them. For we do not know where they run, or who is waiting for them there.

Hathach, stationed near the King's Gate, has also brought me reports every hour or so, and my maids and I sit in my chambers, praying and fasting. He appeared to me near dusk, his tired countenance telling me the fighting was, at last, over.

"Five hundred men have been slaughtered in the palace complex alone, including the ten sons of Haman. The evil of that house is gone."

"And the women and children of our enemies?" I asked.

"They are unharmed, and their worldly goods untouched," Hathach replied.

I leapt to my feet and embraced him, shouting for joy. Our enemies had sought to ruin us, to slit the throat of every child right up to every white-haired elder, and take our possessions as their own. But when my people had been given the ultimate power to inflict revenge, what had they done? Nothing more than justice. G-d's steadying hand has prevailed. My people can be trusted with power.

I knew what I must do next.

My maids and I drank a cup of wine and rubbed a sweet oil on our faces to soften our complexions and give us all a glow of rejoicing. We broke our fast with a hurried meal of dates and fine white bread, but our meal was interrupted, as we anticipated, with a summons to appear before the king.

My robes had been laid out early in the morning, and I was dressed and ready for my king before the moon was at his highest perch in the evening sky. I was anxious to be summoned for a detailed report of the battle, and I did not wait long.

The king had a satisfied look when I approached him.

"Good Queen Esther," he greeted me with a smile, "consider what my messengers have even now told me: In Susa alone, here in the palace complex, five hundred men lay dead who would have raised a sword against your people. Haman's sons lie in the street, and there is no one brave enough to bury them. There is no news yet from the outer provinces, but think of the enemies that are no more and rejoice! Now, what else do you want? Name it and it's yours."

It is a bloody dowry I have brought him, I thought. My thoughts turned to the cities of Sodom and Gomorrah, how their evil had been suppressed but not eliminated, and the final judgment that leveled the city. Evil flourishes best when it has memories. Memories are roots that give rise to a new creature. Little else would matter in the future if we did not secure peace today. There would be no reasoning with our enemies, no ransom. When enemies are bent on massacring you, you must kill them all. It is simple, and true. I want to believe we could make peace with words, but because these men had already sealed our fates in their dreams, we must seal their tombs. We must finish the red chore and be done with it, once for all. And we will send a message to the cowards who had fled before dawn.

"If it please the king," I replied, returning now to our conversation, "have the bodies of Haman's ten sons hanged in public display on the gallows, and let the birds dispose of the bodies as they may. Give the Jews living here inside Susa permission to extend the terms of the order another day. For I am fearful that killing Haman, and his sons, was not enough to dissuade anyone who would dare plot against you, or your throne. Haman's bloodline has ended, but we must be sure his influence is dead as well. Perhaps G-d will yet allow me to repair the breach that King Saul created so long ago."

It took but a moment to summon the scribes of Susa and have the notices printed, sealed, and posted throughout Susa. I wondered about Mordecai and his involvement in the vengeance. He had now been given Haman's position as Chief Adviser to the king. I was anxious to hear the accounts directly from him.

60

Evening, Thirteenth Day of the Month of Adar
Thirteenth Year of the Reign of Xerxes
Year 3405 after Creation

Mordecai has reported to us that seventy-five thousand were killed throughout the province yesterday, and in Susa, an additional three hundred were killed today. Not a single Jew has died during the struggle. I was shocked by the numbers of enemies the Jews have in this land. And yet, how many Jews would have died if Xerxes had not allowed us to defend ourselves? The wind in the garden sounds as if it is sighing, and I wonder how my people feel, knowing now how many were set on their destruction. Throughout the province, Jews have begun celebrating the victory and freedom, and the Jews of Susa have planned a great feast for tomorrow. Mordecai will, no doubt, attend. At dinner tonight, while we drank the royal wine in a room that once saw the man feasting who would destroy us, Mordecai announced his first official act as Chief Adviser:

"If it please the king, and his queen, let notices be written to every Jew throughout the provinces, that these two days will forever be remembered and celebrated in honor of these events, and the bravery of an orphaned girl. The fourteenth and fifteenth days of the month of Adar will be set aside for feasting and laughter, for sending gifts to the poor, and presents to their neighbors. Let the sureness of G-d's hand in unsteady times be blessed forevermore."[1]

"Well done, Mordecai," Xerxes replied. "Your people are indeed a remarkable lot. I could not keep my soldiers from lusting after a fallen enemy's gold, yet your people had my blessing to pillage the enemy, and did not." Xerxes thought on this for a moment before continuing.

"How may I reward your leadership, Mordecai? As my prime minister, the wealth of my kingdom lies before you. What would you take?"

Mordecai raised his palms to the king and shook his head no.

"A woman, then?" Xerxes asked. "A woman from my harem, seasoned over a year before presentation?"

Mordecai laughed out loud. Xerxes found his humble refusal perplexing but laughed as well.

"A feast, then," Xerxes commanded. "A feast that will be as eternal as your devotion to your people, and to Esther. And I proclaim that no one will pay any taxes to the throne in this season, and I will scatter generous gifts among the people. Nothing creates a legend faster than the sound of gold coins in a pocket."

Of course there was never a feast Xerxes didn't love, and the notices went out that night. As Xerxes dictated and sealed the notices,

---

1 Mordecai's notice to all the provinces becomes the basis for the annual Jewish celebration of Purim. The word *purim* comes from the word *pur*, a reference to the dice (then known as *pur*) that Haman tossed to determine the day for the slaughter of the Jews. Purim celebrates the heroism of Esther and the Jewish victory over the evils of genocide, which is why Hitler hated the feast, and Esther, so passionately.

I strolled to the balcony for a taste of the night air in the garden. I glowed with pride to see these two men of vision building a new Persia.

The threat to the throne is gone. Cyrus reports through a note sent to my eunuchs that the will of our enemies is broken as they bury their dead. He does not believe anyone from Haman's plot has lived to remember the vain lust for the throne; he believes the story of the men who escaped at dawn is but a rumor. And of Vashti and Artaxerxes, there is no news. They retreated to another land during the slaughter, and although some of the Immortals went with them, all remains quiet and well since they left.

As I witnessed the night, the many stars brought to mind the many notices that had been posted during Xerxes' reign: of his royal feast after inauguration, of Vashti's banishment and the rule of men, of his call for all virgins to be brought to his harem, and then the destruction of the trapped Jews. And the notices my beauty bought for my people: the right to fight back and overpower an enemy, and to remember forever my name and these times. We had begun the story a distressed people living in borrowed land. How was it possible we now ride on its heights? I was an orphan who could not capture the heart of my first love in the marketplace—how was it I had captured a king, and ruled a nation?

The stars gave me no answers. G-d seemed silent and satisfied. I turned and went back inside to my men, who smiled at me together as they saw my approach. I would ponder my questions another night, perhaps. It is a night for wine and love and justice.

61

Twelfth Day of the Month of Iyyar
Thirteenth Year of the Reign of Xerxes
Year 3406 after Creation

My heart once again has found a steady rhythm after the wild events of days past. I settle in now, and am tending to my affairs as carefully as I once attended my roses. Much of my time has been spent administering Haman's estate. He was a wealthy man, owning many servants and much land. My first concern has been to make sure no child goes unfed here, and that the girls in the provinces grow as freely as any flower on the hills. Women are given more power by my hand; if a man mistreats his wife, or abandons her, she has the power to provide for her family and finish her days in comfort. For I have set Haman's businesses aside for women to run, with orders to employ as many capable women as present themselves. Haman's land and houses make wonderful refuges for women fleeing a harsh husband, or children who need a good meal. In men's hearts I know they still set themselves above us, but I know now that too often we alone bear the burdens of this life, and by my hand, and G-d's providence, no woman need walk alone and ashamed again in this land.

Mordecai has spent so many evenings at the king's side now—it is a wonder I should be jealous of him like a harem girl! Mordecai has loosened the cords that made it uncomfortable for my people to worship in public, to keep to their customs and ways. Together, my two men continue to forge the dream of Persia. Mordecai has already done much to modify the king's plan of taxation, so that everyone pays a proportional share and receives much good. Xerxes has abandoned forever, it seems, his campaigns of war, and sets about campaigns of construction. Roads, seats of government, schools. The people are lavished with stone and bricks, and the finest of engineers from the provinces work through the night on many occasions. I find it interesting that Xerxes has entrusted much power to the people, each in their own regions, and it seems all have adjusted to a reign of peace. The Egyptians roll their eyes at us; they believe stone should be used only for what houses the eternal, such as a tomb. Xerxes counters that if Persia is governed well, she herself will be immortal.

I sleep well at night now, the sweet sleep of a contented laborer, for I believe my most difficult work here is finished. I can enjoy the spoils of my heartache and endeavors, and once again enjoy the gardens, my meals, my king. Yes, I sometimes find my thoughts turning to Cyrus outside my palace door, but the burning that was once lodged in my heart is but a soft warmth, knowing he is as true a friend as he would have been a husband. I did not write my story, but I am grateful for this ending. My people are safe, and many more might now begin their journey toward the homeland unmolested, with the refreshment of hope and quiet days to strengthen them. And if ever there is a girl who cries out for a mother who is not there, she will find refuge under my crown. My name has become a tree that gives shade to the weary.[1]

I am at last free of the unrest that burdened me for so long. I have even taken the custom of writing in this diary in the king's own chambers at night, as I wait for him to return from the court. I rarely even lock it away. And Xerxes often brings papers that his advisers have set before him, and together we discuss their merits before he applies his signet ring. He is amused that I have such instincts for this work and strong intuitions about advisors I never meet.

Once I came to his chambers only when called; now I prefer to leave only when asked. It feels quite comfortable to be at Xerxes' side most every night and to wake with only the sound of his breath and the soft morning cries of the doves in the gardens.

1 Women did indeed prosper at this time. Women enjoyed equal pay for equal work, controlled their own money, and entered into marriages freely with many legal protections. Additionally, although men still hoped their wives gave them sons, the practice of killing female infants was abandoned. New mothers and pregnant women who chose to work were awarded generous rations and pay at the time of birth and during the postpartum recovery.

62

Twenty-sixth Day of the Month of Tammuz
Thirteenth Year of the Reign of Xerxes
Year 3408 after Creation[1]

I returned to my chambers today for a brief respite from Xerxes'
own. It is time for the annual collection of taxes from each province,
and the delegates will assemble in the Throne Hall for an elaborate
display of loyalty and gifts to the crown before having their taxes
counted and entering into the feast Xerxes has commanded. Such
business is not an event for a woman, of course. But a brief respite
will only be good for us both, the way a walk between meals invigo-
rates the appetite.

Yet a strange thing happened today, out of place in this tranquil-
ity only because it was an unfamiliar sight: When I returned to my
chambers, I found Ashtari trying on one of my robes and surveying

---

1 Once again, a gap of dates appears in the diaries. This one is approximately
three years, and two entries later, a second gap of four years appears. However,
new evidence suggests that this particular scroll once included the missing dates.
Someone removed a portion of the diary; perhaps it was a contemporary who
wanted to hide their own role in the events of her life, or it was done at a later
date, either by accident or with malice. Esther's voice is remarkable in that no
regime, and no leader, has been able to silence her.

herself in the polished mirror. She was deeply shamed and filled with words of remorse when she finally saw me watching her, and I forgave her this one indiscretion. I have been careless, thoughtless, to live with such splendor for myself and not think she would grow to yearn. Poor, loving Ashtari. I resolve to share more of my treasures with her. Never was a friend as constant and steady in times of trouble, and I have not rewarded her as such. But I will begin.

63

Eleventh Day of the Month of Kislev
Thirteenth Year of the Reign of Xerxes
Year 3408 after Creation

My once unrestrained joy is tempered now by the weary truth of days without change, for still I am not pregnant. Xerxes has perhaps set aside this dream; but of course, his harem girls and minor wives have provided him with heirs many times over. Indeed, his firstborn son, Artaxerxes, continues to be a source of worry among the court.

So is it a matter of pride that I still long to carry a child? Am I of no value if I remain barren? That is the opinion of some in the court; I can feel their cold stares as I return to the king's chambers night after night. They do not understand what use the king has for a woman who can give him nothing. It is true—I have not given Xerxes a son so that his name would be carried on. But I gave Xerxes a name that would be carried on because of honor and not infamy. How I have so often stopped him from running to disaster and opened to him the hearts of a foreign people. Yes, my spirit has done more for this man than my womb ever could. Must I always apologize for this barrenness when I am in the courts?

Yet it is my womb that feels its emptiness above all, and she cannot be consoled, even with the great things I have done. I have begged G-d night and day, but why He would open the heavens on so many occasions but remain silent on this one requires a faith beyond my own. I walk these great halls with the certainty that I rule here, but my will falters. I find it hard to pray every day, every morning, to have the rabbi offer sacrifices on my behalf, and yet receive no word in return, no blessing. Did I fail in my great task, my Lord? Why do You not answer and so provoke me to wrath? Would it not be sin to be angry with You now, after You have delivered me through so much, and then delivered a nation through me? Can we not come to peace on this, my G-d? Can You not grant me a child, and so satisfy this crippling longing? Or if not, can You not give me an answer, and so set my heart at rest? How long, O Lord, will I wait for either? I drive myself mad asking these questions at every moment.

Were it not for the comfort of true friends, and the satisfaction of a palace governed by the Lord's hand, I would not sleep so deeply, and enjoy the pleasures G-d does see fit to grant me. I can even content myself that it is Xerxes' name that is recorded in the annals of the historians, not mine, and yet it is through me that a new world of peace and fair government is born.

I smiled as I wrote that sentence. Sometimes, when I am writing, it is as if I feel the breath of G-d across the page. I have not given the king an heir, and my womb remains empty, but through me peace at last entered Persia. I gave birth to something beautiful in this world; am I not a mother then? It is a beautiful answer to the questions in my heart tonight.

And I will end with this: Like a mother, I worry for her, this precious peace. When I am gone, what will happen to her, this peace of Persia?

64

*Twenty-second Day of the Month of Shevat
Twentieth Year of the Reign of Xerxes
Year 3412 after Creation*

Cyrus is dead.

There are so few details, and Ashtari was pained to tell me of them all. She knew Cyrus was loyal to me, even above the throne, but she knew nothing else of him. How good of her to shield me from what more she must know of his death. It seems that he was struck down when he confronted a group of men near the Gate of All Nations. Probably thieves, Ashtari reports. No one saw the men closely or can report more details than that.

Tragedy always travels with her twin sister, however. After Cyrus's death, his men, the men most loyal to him throughout Haman's intrigue, died in an accident. They had gone together to the local temple, perhaps to offer sacrifices to Ahura Mazda in Cyrus's memory, and to ease their grief. Together they went to a lower chamber, a private quarter made available to them by the ruling Magi. As they gathered, a channel in the aqueduct burst suddenly, filling the small room with water immediately. No one survived. Indeed, no one above would even have heard their cries for help. Is it fitting, I wonder, that they all died in silence? Even Cyrus's death is muted by the slim account Ashtari can give. No one ever knew who Cyrus was to me. Not even Mordecai. How odd he would have loomed so large in my life, and so small in others' eyes.

So he is gone. There is a long scar across my heart where his name once was written. I had seared it away after so many nights in Xerxes' bed, willing myself to love the man G-d had brought me, and not the one I had yearned for. I would have expected this news to rip the flesh of my heart apart, but as I waited to feel the searing pain, I felt only a deep sadness in my spirit. My friend was gone, and for him I would grieve, but I knew now my love had died so many years ago, and I no longer grieve for him in that way. Oh, Cyrus, how many burdens you surely bore of your own, that I knew nothing of. We were strangers who knew each other's memory so well. I wish you speed to the arms of the eternal G-d, and rest among the fathers of our people. You were truly the bravest of us all, and the only constant good in a world of fools. May G-d fill you now with the love you were denied on earth, may your name be blessed, and may the hand that slew you be damned for eternity.

65

Fourth Day of the Month of Av
Twenty-second Year of the Reign of Xerxes
Year 3414 after Creation

I awoke to the sounds of crying in the dark hours of morning. I had returned to my own chambers the evening before, to wait for the time of my menstrual bleeding to pass. Ashtari stood over my bed, weeping. I looked about in alarm to see what had disturbed her so, but no one else was in my chambers. Something was out of place, and the odd peace shook me awake.

"What is it, Ashtari?" I implored. "What has happened?"

She could only cry and look at me with a desolation I had not seen in her eyes before. "I am sorry, my queen. Forgive your servant," she said quietly. As she dabbed at her eyes, a stunning jewel of size on her finger sparkled even in the dim moonlight.

My blood ran cold. "What have you done, Ashtari?" I asked.

She shook her head, and choked out her last words to me, "Go and see your king. You must hurry before the end."

As I wrapped my chamber robes around me quickly, she shoved a satchel in my hands. Not waiting for an escort, I threw open my chamber door. Hagai's body slumped against my shins as I stepped out. He had been run through with a sword, his entrails bulging against the wound. I screamed and flew down the halls until at last I was in Xerxes' chambers. There were no guards posted at the entrance, and no one was attending him. It was as if all were dead.

Xerxes lay on his bed, gasping for breath. He smiled a moment when he saw me alive, but his eyes began to close even as I took his hand.

"No, no, Xerxes, you cannot die! What has happened?" I cried. "Who has done this to you?"

He rolled his head to see me more clearly as thick spittle ran out of his mouth. It had a sharp odor. "Is it too late, Esther?" he gasped.

I shook my head in confusion and wiped his brow. My tears fell against the linens on the bed, mixing with his vomit and sweat.

He tried again. "I want G-d. Your G-d. But I am a man of lust, of idols."

"Go to him, Xerxes." My tears were falling too fast; it was hard for me to talk as well, but I smiled for him, one last smile between lovers. "I have told Him all about you. He says to tell you all will be forgiven; only come home now."

Xerxes labored for a last breath, and as he exhaled, he told me nothing more but asked a question. "Did you love me, my Star?"

"Never more than I do now, my good king."

With that, he died. I sat, seeing myself smooth down his covers and touch his face, but unable to master my movements. It was as if someone else was moving my limbs for me. I had the oddest sensation of not being there, of being in a dream. I looked at the floor near the door and realized I had dropped the bundle that Ashtari had shoved to me. It had spilled open, and I could see my diary and a little necklace. It called to me, and as I stared mutely at it, I found its voice, for it was the necklace given to me as a girl by a friend from the market. I had worn it the morning I had been taken from my home to serve in the harem. Ashtari had sent me with the things most dear to me, what I had brought into this palace as a girl. To see them now was like seeing a ghost, the one who comes at night when the old ones are dying, to take their hand for the eternal journey. A little scrap of papyrus caught my eye, for it did not belong. It was not of my hand. I held it to the light and read:

Forgive me, Esther, and remember me when you go to your G-d. I have only done what I must to buy my freedom from this place. I served you well for all the years you were here. It is only at the end I find I must betray you, but you have led a good and high life. You gave your youth to the king and were so generously rewarded. I gave my youth to you, and now wait with open palms. You cannot begrudge me a brief happiness before my years on earth are over. How ironic that a Jew forced me to this place, and I must now force a Jew from it.

Do not be shocked that your servant can write and read. I chose never to tell you, for reading your diaries gave me access to people and places a servant cannot go. I knew who would be for me, and who would oppose me. The men who slipped away at dawn are my brothers, who came to Susa to rescue me long ago, but found they, too, had to wait for the seasons to change.

In another land they were united with a powerful ally,
who arrives tonight to return to the throne. I do not
wish this next evil on you; I only wish you gone.
   I know that you loved me as a sister, and for this
affection I granted you a good-bye with your king. But
all is finished, and you must ready yourself for the end.

So it was done. It's strange that anger has left me, and I find a peace drawing near to me, all around, that grants me the strength to forgive even now. I forgive them. I forgive Ashtari most of all, for she has betrayed me more than most. I do not know if the others, the many who have served me in this palace, are alive or dead, but I will bless them, too. For some of them no doubt loved and yet betrayed, and am I no different? For it seems now I gave my heart only twice in my life, and both times it was too late. We are a fumbling lot, a humanity that distorts the echo of the divine.

I have fled to a deeper chamber of the palace. I found a pen and began to write. If this is indeed the doing of Artaxerxes, they will be coming for me soon. I am truly to die barren, I know that now, but I must plant a seed to bear fruit for a new generation.[1]

---

1 This date of this entry appears to be two years later, indicating again a gap in the diaries and placing the murder of Xerxes on a different date than some scholars have suggested. The murder of Xerxes was recorded by the royal historians; readers may refer to the Babylonian Astronomical Text. However, because there were three different prominent cultures within the empire, each using a separate calendar, the date given for Xerxes' execution seems at first to differ between accounts. Babylonian, Hebrew, and Egyptian calendars began recording a new reign only after the next new year, but each marked the new year in different months. The differing dates between scholars have been attributed to these different calendar schemes. A team including forensic archaeologists and epigraphists who have worked on the Dead Sea Scrolls and the ossuary of James has been retained to study the gaps in the diaries; perhaps in later years we will have an answer as to who removed portions of the diary—and why.

66

You have heard my story and been my faithful companion down these darkened catacombs of the buried past. Of course we are all gone now. My time to die is upon me; my beauty was, indeed, fleeting. My husband, the great King Xerxes, is dead as well. There was much speculation during his reign that his death would be deliberate at the hands of his enemies. Had he seen beyond his cups he might have known who they were and how best to stop them. But the man whose appetites had ruled a nation was ultimately consumed by death itself.

I long to tell you more, and hear your own story, but my time with you has come to an end. My hand, once so smooth and sure as it wrote across these pages, has grown frightened and faltering. I doubt Mordecai has survived this night. My time is truly done. How blessed I am to at last shrug off my burdens, this world of sand and tears, to see the face of the Christ[1] and lay my coveted crown at the feet of the King of Kings.

---

1 Jews referred to their hoped-for Savior as the Christ, the Greek translation of this word being used for this edition. When Jesus arrived about five hundred years later, many Jews recognized him as the Christ, and so Jesus became known as the Christ Jesus, or Jesus Christ.

The guards are coming to these chambers now; I can hear their movements in the palace. I will find a friend among them to remove this diary and set it in the tomb of the ancients here in Persia. They betrayed Xerxes' crown for gold; they will betray the new and coming king for such as well. Their greed gives me peace, for I know that for the right price, my scrolls will be safely carried away. I will tell them I have set a spy among the people; if the scrolls are not well hidden, the guard will be killed. (It is a lie, but I trust it will be forgiven.) I will bless this diary before it leaves me, my faithful companion for these many years, and pray that it journeys someday to another woman of destiny. It must not be wasted on women who do not have the ears to hear the soft call of G-d, or the eyes to see beyond their own reflections. I will pray that no one will find this story, except for another woman who has been called. I pray to embrace you, my dear one, when we meet on G-d's shores someday. You have come to know me so well in these pages. I smile to think that I will know you as well when we meet in eternity.

Now your own time has come: What is your future? Why has G-d brought you to a time such as this? I wonder what evil will rise in your time; it is said that if you cut off the head of a snake, two more will grow in its place. Haman is but dust now, yet evil is alive. The serpent lives to strike another woman, in another time. I pray you will have faith in G-d for those evil days, and faithful friends to turn to. Your effect on the world will be immediate, and eternal.

Go now. Go to your future. Let my story, and the words of G-d's Holy Scriptures, give you comfort and strength for what must be done. When your victory is assured, and you raise a cup of wine at your own feast, look to the stars and give me a smile. For who can change the world quite like a woman?[2]

---

2 See commentary on page 288 of the appendix.

APPENDIX

COMMENTS ON THE LOST DIARIES

M. C. ROSENBLUM, CURATOR OF THE LOST DIARIES

"THE WOMEN OF THE BIBLE: OUR SISTERS, OUR SELVES"

WOMEN'S VIEW LECTURE SERIES, BOSTON

SEPTEMBER 18, 2004

Queen Vashti was considered to be the most beautiful woman in the empire. This claim is never disputed, even in light of the events that will soon transpire in this story. Esther will need moral courage for the days soon ahead, but she will need another kind of courage as well: the belief that her beauty is a reflection of God's inspired appeal. Esther lived in a world that judged women solely by appearance. If Esther believes in the standards of her time, and judges herself by them, she will not be able to do what lies ahead for her.

What was it that set Esther apart? Although we do not know how Mordecai allowed Esther to groom herself, we know her peers used cosmetics to increase their allure. Fats from animals such as lions and crocodiles were used as the base for cosmetics and perfumes, and it was believed that the strength and beauty of these animals would be passed along to the wearers. These fats, mixed with color, lined the eyes and lips, and were applied based on the premise that light always creates highlights and shadows. To be alluring as a woman, one must draw the eye to a good feature, and away from a lesser one.

The Jews say God created Esther with a different approach. Esther's peers used cosmetics to manipulate the light around them. Yet, fashioned by God, in this story Esther would *be* the light. It is taught that women are illuminated internally by His power and strength. He has shaped them to His satisfaction. They are a reflection of the supernatural.

Queen Vashti was indeed considered the most beautiful woman in the empire. God would not have Esther challenge that in the days ahead. Instead, God would have Esther become the most powerful woman in the empire and a beloved woman of history. The Jews believe she was not created to embody the fashion of her times, but to reflect the majesty and providence of a God moving unseen through the world, even the forgotten world of women.

COMMENTS ON THE LOST DIARIES

M. C. ROSENBLUM, CURATOR OF THE LOST DIARIES, CONTINUED

A leading criminal behavior expert once said, "By the time a girl has reached her teens, she has gone from being an occasional sexual predatory prize to the leading sexual predatory prize."[1]

Yes, the cloak of childhood has protected Esther until now. As she prepares to enter womanhood, she must prepare for new dangers as well. As girls mature into women, they must face the threat that some men seek to harm them. Preparing a girl for the worst kind of danger, while giving her freedom, is a chasm most parents find difficult to cross.

FOR IMMEDIATE RELEASE

OFFICE OF THE PRESS SECRETARY

SEPTEMBER 23, 2003

PRESIDENT BUSH ADDRESSES THE UNITED NATIONS ASSEMBLY

THE UNITED NATIONS

NEW YORK, NEW YORK

The President:

"Events during the past two years have set before us the clearest of divides: between those who seek order, and those who spread chaos; between those who work for peaceful change, and those who adopt the methods of gangsters; between those who honor the rights of man, and those who deliberately take the lives of men and women and children without mercy or shame.

"There's another humanitarian crisis spreading, yet hidden from view. Each year, an estimated 800,000 to 900,000 human beings are bought, sold, or forced across the world's borders. Among them are hundreds of thousands of teenage girls, and others as young as five, who fall victim to the sex trade. This commerce in human life generates billions of dollars each year ...

"There's a special evil in the abuse and exploitation of the most innocent and vulnerable. The victims of the sex trade see little of life before they see the very worst of life—an underground of brutality and lonely fear. Those who create these victims and profit from their suffering must be severely punished. Those who patronize this industry debase themselves and deepen the misery of others. And governments that tolerate this trade are tolerating a form of slavery.

"The American government is committing $50 million to support the good work of organizations that are rescuing women and children from exploitation, and giving them shelter and medical treatment and the hope of a new life. We must show new energy in fighting an old evil … the trade in human beings for any purpose must not be allowed to thrive in our time."

COMMENTS ON THE LOST DIARIES
M. C. ROSENBLUM, CURATOR OF THE LOST DIARIES, CONTINUED

Esther has entered, for the first time, a world in which her body is not her own. It will be judged, critiqued, and manipulated every day that she awakens in the harem. Our modern lives are not so different, are they? When even the most beautiful movie star is judged too imperfect for the cover of a magazine without extensive photo airbrushing and retouches, how can we be comfortable with our own, more humble, imperfections?

Esther's story begins with her awareness, not of her great beauty, but of her imperfections. She will grow in power by embracing the imperfections all around her, in herself, and in others. This is the lesson, then, of Esther's imperfections: When we risk letting down our guard and taking off our masks, when we let others see our weaknesses and faults, we draw them to us. We send out a quiet signal that it's safe to be real with us. Her power, and ours, does not grow by comparing our beauty to another's, or by insisting our strength is superior, but by setting all claims aside.

ANDY STANLEY, AUTHOR: *VISIONEERING*

Do you wake up every day to circumstances that have absolutely nothing remotely to do with the vision you sense God developing in you? Then you are in good company. Joseph reviewed his vision from an Egyptian dungeon. Moses spent years following sheep. David, the teenage king, spent years hiding in caves. And Nehemiah was the cupbearer to the very king whose ancestors had destroyed the city he longed to rebuild! Be encouraged. God has you there for a reason.... I would guess the time required for God to grow you into his vision for your life will be somewhere between four months and forty years.... There seems to be a correlation between the preparation time and the magnitude of the task.[2]

COMMENTS ON THE LOST DIARIES

M. C. ROSENBLUM, CURATOR OF THE LOST DIARIES, CONTINUED

Esther had no political or personal power over her fate. Her only bargaining chip was to conceive a child, preferably a boy. Bearing the king's child would afford her better accommodations in the wives' harem and preferential treatment for the rest of her days. In fact, Esther's job was to make herself so luscious that the king would want to sleep with her repeatedly, thereby increasing her chances of conceiving. Esther's sexuality was centered on two goals: pleasing the man and producing a child. Fertility was literally worshipped in her era; sexuality was the means to an end.

The message to Esther and her peers was that the key to happiness lies in seducing a man, because a seductive woman had more chances for children, and surely women who were mothers were, indeed, a happier lot.

For us, Esther's modern sisters, our sex-to-children equation is almost completely inverse to her own. Esther's generation welcomed sex with the right man because it offered a chance for pregnancy, and motherhood gave them social and economic advancement. But today, the message to modern women is that they must avoid getting pregnant so that they can continue to have plenty of sex with many partners, because surely women who do this are a happier lot.

Esther dared to go against the blatant dictates of culture. She did not view her sexuality as a commodity that might afford her a better life. She was emotionally detached from the promises of the harems and the king. She believed that nothing, and no one, could offer her anything that didn't come first and best from the hands of her almighty God. Her culture did not determine her behavior, nor did her devastating need for protection and provision. She was a woman enslaved who was completely free. And it is only when we dare set our faces against the winds of our culture, to take the more difficult path, that our names are remembered and celebrated throughout the generations.

EXCERPT FROM ADDRESS TO HOLY INNOCENTS PREPARATORY SCHOOL

M. C. ROSENBLUM, CURATOR OF THE LOST DIARIES

DALLAS, TEXAS

NOVEMBER 12, 2004

Look around you. Doesn't it seem that today's girls, like Esther, live in a harem? They have more freedom of movement, but are the standards and expectations so different? Every girl wants to catch the eye of "the king." Every girl is offering up her wares and looking at other girls with a wary eye. And like the women in Esther's harem, they feel sure that if they could only catch the eye of this elusive king, they would be moved up to a better life, and a better place.

Every other woman took something of value into Xerxes' bedchamber for their introduction, whether it was his favorite food, or an exotic dance they had learned with seductive props, or a treasure from their homeland. Esther brought only herself, esteeming herself as the best gift she could offer. But she would not lay herself down on his bed, dreaming of what this encounter would mean for her future. She knew this king had nothing in his palace, or his treasuries, to offer in exchange for her purity. It was a gift too costly even for the vast sums of wealth he held.

Esther carried herself in honor and was given more. Honor wins more honor. The girls who honored seduction as their only asset got only sex. Esther valued herself, and her God above all, and was given the kingdom and the king.

ADDRESS TO THE WOMEN'S CAUCUS OF FINDING FREEDOM: SOCIOECONMOMIC SOLUTIONS FOR WOMEN

M. C. ROSENBLUM, CURATOR OF THE LOST DIARIES

SAN DIEGO, CA

OCTOBER 6, 2004

> *As I saw that hand and foot, something irrational happened: a lifetime's orientation toward maternal rights over fetal rights lurched out of kilter. Some voice from the most primitive core of my brain—the voice of the species?—said: You must protect that little hand at all costs; no harm can come to it or its owner. That little hand, that small human signature, is more important now than you are. The message was unambivalent.*[3]

These are the words of a staunchly pro-choice woman as she describes seeing, for the first time, an ultrasound image of her unborn child. She calls it an "irrational experience," this realization that an unborn baby may indeed have greater priority than she had imagined.

Now think of a drugstore, any drugstore in any city in the United States. The family-planning aisle is a row overwhelmed with products. If you can't find what you like, a prescription can get you anything from behind the counter as well. Creams, pills, diaphragms, IUDs, sponges, condoms, patches, injections—not to mention all the surgical procedures available at any nearby hospital and clinic. For the first time in the history of the Western world, a woman's choices are limitless. We can determine our behavior, control many of the foreseeable consequences, and no longer fear condemnation. We can choose when to become sexually active, and with whom. We can choose to remain faithful in a marriage, or have affairs. We can choose from any number of methods to prevent or encourage conception.

Esther and her peers had no choices. They would never have "partners"; they would be with one man, their husband, and he would be chosen for them. Contraception was limited; most notably, crocodile feces packed in as a barrier method.

The real debate today isn't about our choices; it's about our honor. The fight for women's rights has given us much, but hasn't yet called us to greater glory. Our victories threaten to strip us of honor, for we seem unwilling to accept responsibility for our choices. We are becoming less than we were created to be. We have pursued women's rights until they have become women's whims. We must not let our choices lead us to indulgence; may our choices lead us to integrity, and our integrity lead us to honor.

WOMEN AND TERROR: A NEW UNDERSTANDING OF THE WAR

M. C. ROSENBLUM, CURATOR OF THE LOST DIARIES

With wars and terror attacks increasingly claiming the lives of civilians, civilian interest and involvement in peace strategy is more intense than in any previous generation. War has become intensely personal, claiming the lives of innocents at restaurants, parks, on public transportation.

But just as terrorism is a war waged by individuals, peace is becoming the work of individuals as well.

Women in particular are effective at creating peace. Accustomed to being ignored by mainstream war policy, women are used to considering alternative strategies, tools, and methods that curb hatred and violence.

Women have lived with terrorism in a deeply personal way, being forced to always consider the risks inherent in dark parking lots, empty streets, and walking unescorted through certain neighborhoods. Terrorism in the form of rape and violent, impersonal attack has shaped how women live from the moment they are born. Now that awareness of terrorism has at last become an international issue, women are uniquely qualified to offer solutions.

Women's solutions tend to be immediate, practical, and independent of government agency. Policy has never protected a woman in a dark alley, and peace has never lasted as long as the human heart is capable of harboring hate. Women understand the impersonal reality of hatred and violence, the complete lack of logic behind acts of terrorism, and the dangerous, difficult work that peace is. Women at the negotiating table may offer the best hope we have for ending the violence that has shattered families and scorched cities.

"[Wisdom] has prepared her meat and mixed her wine; she has also set her table," says Proverbs 9:2. In Proverbs, wisdom is personified as a woman, and here we see her setting the table for a feast. You could make the case that this is classic literary foreshadowing in the Bible, since Proverbs was written about three hundred years before Esther lived. Let's focus on the message.

Jesus taught His disciples a foundational truth about life: If you are faithful with the little things, you can be trusted with even greater things. It's so easy to want to jump to greatness without having done all of the footwork. Is it possible, here in this moment, you are being rehearsed for greatness, tested to see if you know how to use the little things God has entrusted you with?

You could argue that Esther had only been entrusted with the littlest of little things: clothes, makeup, jewelry, confined in a palace to serve the whims of a pagan king. And on the eve of the greatest Jewish genocide the world had yet seen, she did not abandon what she had been given. She did not call down from heaven for resources beyond what she already had; she called down from heaven and asked that what she had been entrusted with would be enough.

She hosted a dinner party. She dressed up. She dabbed on her perfume and placed her jewelry. It's what she had, and it's what she used. And she was about to become one of the greatest women in history.

When you are frustrated with your circumstances, when you feel you are being held back, perhaps God is keeping you there because

He doesn't want you to overlook the little things. Abraham Lincoln once said, "The doors of history swing on small hinges." Your job today is to embrace the insignificant. Accept life when it seems to go in slow motion. Pay attention to the mundane, and the humble. They may be your greatest assets when your own divine moment of truth is revealed.

No one knows how Esther or Mordecai died. King Xerxes was buried in a tomb carved into a mountain, just outside of Persepolis. He was laid to rest with his father, Darius. Little is known of what became of the other women of his harem, or his many wives. Popular Iranian legend has it that Esther and Mordecai were buried together in the town of Hamadan. Religious pilgrims and tourists visit this site almost daily to pay respects to the fallen hero and heroine.

Although King Xerxes was assassinated, scholars debate whether the evidence points to his son, Artaxerxes, as the assassin. Ironically, Artaxerxes was himself poisoned, as were his sons. Artaxerxes assumed the throne but would never recapture the glory of his father's empire; indeed, his reign began the freefall decline of the Persian Empire. Revolts and insurrections would surface. While Artaxerxes and his successors would busy themselves with defending the kingdom, hoofbeats could be heard in the distance, for the time of Alexander the Great was quickly approaching.

... a little more ...

When a delightful concert comes to an end,

the orchestra might offer an encore.

When a fine meal comes to an end,

it's always nice to savor a bit of dessert.

When a great story comes to an end,

we think you may want to linger.

And so, we offer ...

AfterWords—just a little something more after you

have finished a David C. Cook novel.

We invite you to stay awhile in the story.

Thanks for reading!

Turn the page for ...

- **A Sneak Peak**
  - **Q&A**
  - **Notes**
- **About the Author**

Sneak Peek

THE LOST LOVES SERIES
BOOK TWO

You who hesitate, cast aside all illusions.

—Abba Kovner

PROLOGUE

He saw the spirit only briefly, a glimpse of its dark hair and slight body moving silently through the forest. He had known it was there before he saw it. The hair on his arms had raised, and he held up a hand to the men following behind him, who all drew their horses to a quick stop. Birds called above them, and monkeys fled from lower branches to the higher perches. A few threw fruit at the men. A lion growled and they could hear his steps. They held their breath until they knew he was moving in another direction.

When the lion's steps grew faster and fainter, he knew the spirit had come. The unknowing men stooped and retrieved the fruit, laughing at the ones who had reached for their swords too quickly. He saw the spirit in that moment, her bow drawn tight against the gutstring, sliding between the trees in front of him. She lifted her head to draw the scent from the wind and let her arrow fly. Then she ran.

He jumped from his horse and followed. The forest was nothing like his arid home, and he tripped and fell as vines caught his ankles and branches slapped his face. He tried to move faster and leap higher, but the forest had broken many rash men and she prevailed again. Panting, he leaned against a tree.

He had heard the land in the north worshipped a goddess, one who hunted and killed, then loved and birthed, but he had never imagined she would seduce a man so perfectly at a glance. Her magic wove its way into his flesh, biting and burrowing, devouring weaker memories of love and promises made. He held up his hand and looked at it as the leaves above parted with a breeze to allow the sun a view.

His skin was pristine. He looked unchanged.

"Our bodies lie until age forces them to tell the truth," he whispered. "Keep then my secret from my men so that I will not be made a fool."

He staggered back to his men, torn and bleeding, and resumed the journey north.

That night he slept close to the fire, and the forest fog stole around the men as they made camp, blanketing them in the way of the wild, that bitter mother, who welcomes and warns in the same caress. Darkness was alive here. Eyes blinked from behind the trees. Throats opened and sang. Footsteps broke through vines and dead wood as the creatures drew closer to smell the men and horses. The horses snorted and circled.

A thick brew was passed around, an elixir they called "saddle cure" because of its powerful magic that put a trail-weary explorer to sleep in minutes and soothed sore muscles. The next morning they would feel worse for drinking it, but no man on the trail thinks of tomorrow. The lions crawling through the underbrush nearby reminded them there may be no need.

So Ahab drew nearest the fire and let the other men take the outer edges of camp to sleep. He felt a few sparks land too near and brushed them away. He would rather suffer a small singe than a bigger bite. Life as a king meant weighing which pain should get preference. Ahab had grown up watching his father get devoured by the needling little wars of politics even as he crushed armies. King Omri had been dead for two weeks, and Ahab knew the world was changed. The wars for new land were over; now men would die for gold … and gold alone. His first bold move as the warrior king of Israel would be tomorrow, when he claimed a bride he did not want.

He had gone on many such journeys with his father to claim lands and peoples. It was a simple matter: He who struck first and hardest, won. The sword was impartial to temperaments and whims. Politics and war were alike in that neither gave room for desire; all was won and weighed by leverage. So it was with this expedition. A princess would be given as a treaty between the kingdoms, and the kingdoms would unite against the savage Assyrians growing in power along the borders, who would go to war for the trade routes in the heartland.

Ahab was not pleased to take a wife. He had a harem of women he could call on to serve him and then be silent. A wife was a burden he was ill equipped to handle, for what arguments could be solved with the sword? He lived for blood, not love. But this woman was a necessary cost. Ahab spit into the fire thinking of it. The fire didn't blink and his gesture was lost. Ahab sighed and turned over.

It was deep into the night when the sparks singed him along his arms. The first one was so slight that Ahab only acknowledged its victory in his mind and went back to sleep. The heat from the fire had kept the night bugs away but made him too warm to sleep in his clothes, so he slept naked, covering only the essentials with his blanket. Then the sparks came more frequently, spitting and poking into his exposed skin along the thick part of his arms and chest. Finally he sat up in disgust, determined to move away from the fire's reach.

The fire was only glowing embers now. There were no sparks.

He heard a soft laugh catch in a throat, and he reached for his sword. A hand shot from the darkness and caught his. The creature edged closer and smiled. Ahab froze. Her eyes were large black hollows. Her lips were dark and sharply edged, though full through the middle. And she was beautiful. The moonlight made her pale olive skin look like polished marble, and he wondered if she would return to stone by morning. The goddess crawled across the dust and dead sparks. She dropped the arrow she had used to rouse him.

He drew back, holding his breath, arranging the blanket where it was suddenly needed. Her long fingers moved across his face, and she closed her eyes when she touched his mouth. She breathed deeply, then looked at him. Her arm moved to her belt and brought up a knife, which she brought to his face. He could not move. No man in the camp made any sound beyond snoring and turning. She released his hand and crawled closer so that her knees were against his hip. She lifted a section of his hair and cut it loose, returning the knife to her belt and the hair to a pouch next to it. She looked at him again now and waited. She did not blink.

He remembered a dream he had once, as a boy, of falling. In this dream, he fell from a very safe place into a deep, cold well where no one could hear him. He remembered how every revolution, every stone that passed by as he fell into the darkness, marked the dark descent. When he awoke that morning, he saw he had only fallen from the bed as he slept, but he cried anyway. He had wiped his tears with vigor so that his servant Obadiah would have nothing to report to his harsh father at breakfast.

But now he fell and did not dream. He moved his hands to the small of her back and felt her strong frame, moving his hands up her back to the shoulders and drawing her face to his now. He saw the lines of her mouth split into a smile, and he kissed her. He held her there, and she released a soft breath into his mouth. He swallowed and kissed her again, then reached to pull her on top of him. She slipped from his grasp and stole back into the darkness, like a little songbird that only needed a moment's distraction to make its escape.

He lay back on the earth and cried.

Q&A

WITH GINGER GARRETT

Q: Why did you include *Chosen: The Lost Diaries of Queen Esther* in the David C. Cook series Lost Loves of the Bible?

A: I chose these diaries for the Lost Loves series because of the potential for love that Esther lost.

The moment Esther was chosen for the harem, whatever hopes she had for her future, her heart, and her family were lost. She became one wife among thousands. She lost freedom and many days, she lost her dignity in the treatment she received.

However, Esther is foreshadowing the story of Christ, who tells us that to surrender our own desires and plans will lead to blessings unimaginable, and overflow goodness into the lives of others. Esther's loss, and her submission to a cruel turn of events, resulted in the saving of a nation. Millions of Jews were saved throughout history by her sacrifices.

Q: What are the other books in the Lost Loves series?

A: I'll be adding two novels: the stories of Jezebel and Delilah. Both women have been sorely overlooked by history, painted as cardboard villains without any understanding of who they were and why they acted as they did. Their stories are more poignant, and disturbing, than what we've ever imagined.

Q: Will you ever complete the Serpent Moon series?

A: Since I get this question every day on email from readers, I thought I'd answer it here, too!

Dark Hour began what was to be a trilogy of evil women from the Bible. However, due to circumstances well beyond my control, I had to stop work on the series, while certain events sorted themselves out.

While I won't be returning to the trilogy, I will be returning to my desire to tell the stories of two epic women from biblical history: Jezebel and Delilah. Their stories, their passions, and the loves they lost compel me to finish the work.

It's fitting, really, that these women be allowed to tell their tales without the stigma of being in a series about evil women of the Bible. Until we get past that label, and see their hearts, we can't begin to understand the lessons they would whisper to us across the generations that separate us.

NOTES

1   Gavin de Becker, *Protecting the Gift* (New York: Random House, 1999), 30–33.

2   Andy Stanley, *Visioneering* (Sisters, Oregon: Multnomah, 1999), 24.

3   Naomi Wolf, *Misconceptions* (New York: Doubleday, 2001), 28.

ABOUT THE AUTHOR

Ginger Garrett is the author of the Chronicles of the Scribes series (*In the Shadow of Lions, In the Arms of Immortals, In the Eyes of Eternity*), *Dark Hour*, and *Beauty Secrets of the Bible*. *Chosen: The Lost Diaries of Queen Esther* was recognized as one of the top five novels of 2006 by the ECPA.

Focusing on ancient women's history, Ginger creates novels and nonfiction resources that explore the lives of historical women. A frequent media guest and television host, Ginger has been interviewed by Fox News, Billy Graham's *The Hour of Decision, The Harvest Show*, 104.7 The Fish Atlanta, and many other outlets.

A graduate of Southern Methodist University with a degree in theater, she is passionate about creating art from history.

Visit Ginger at her Web site: www.gingergarrett.com
Author photo © Don Sparks Photography

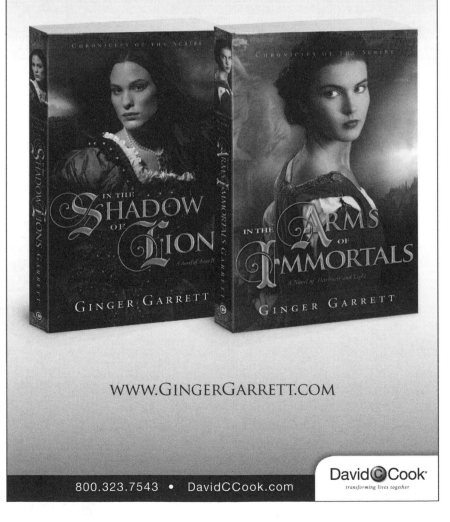